INTERSECTIONS

INTERSECTIONS

Short Stories from Rideshare Passengers

By Andrew Spink

Audacity Press

A division of Audacity

Library of Congress Control Number (LCCN): 2022923298

ISBN: 979-8-9874521-0-3

979-8-9874521-1-0 (hardcover) | 979-8-9874521-2-7 (ebook)

First Audacity hardcover edition: March 2023
First Audacity trade paperback edition: February 2023

Cover Art: Tracy Simpson | Tracy-Simpson.com
Cover Design: Audacity

For the amazing people behind the characters. Thank you for sharing yourselves with us all.

CONTENTS

PROLOGUE

Janelle was shell-shocked, her face locked in position - eyebrows raised, jaw dropped, a partial smile. Four minutes into her airport trip, they were stopping to pick up a second passenger, and it just happened to be *him*. She racked her brain, trying to think of the last time she'd seen him. The last time they'd spoken. The last time they kissed.

James' knees buckled as he reached for the door handle. His whole body felt numb. Here he was, thousands of miles from home, about to take an Uber to the airport, and he couldn't believe his eyes. There, sitting in the back seat, staring back at him with equal astonishment, was his high school sweetheart - sixteen years after graduation.

The universe had done something special. Something magical. Out of all the possibilities for where life could've taken them, here they were - on the opposite coast from where they'd met, so many years later, and yet somehow sharing my backseat for an afternoon ride to the airport.

James and Janelle had been as in love as any fourteen-year-olds could be. All throughout high school, they found every excuse to be near each other. To flirt. To let their forearms graze each other. The only complication was Janelle's religious family. James was Catholic, but Janelle's family were devout Baptists, and she was forbidden to date him. She wasn't allowed to date anyone, actually, so they had to sneak around, stealing kisses when they were alone and perfecting the art of holding hands without being spotted.

After graduation, their lives diverged. James stayed in Buffalo and Janelle headed west. They only caught glimpses of each other on Facebook, or in occasional dreams and doppelgangers on the street, and once at the wedding of a mutual friend four years ago, where they locked eyes but couldn't bring themselves to even say "hi." Janelle was accompanied by her husband and kids, and James was with his fiancée. And so, even though it was years later, and their love had become a distant memory, there was something unspoken between the two of them. Some spark deemed too dangerous for a conversation. They didn't want to tempt fate.

Over the twenty-minute ride to the airport, Janelle and James picked up right where their teenage selves had left off. They shared memories of soccer matches and cross-country races. They re-lived the highlights of marching in the band or playing in the wind ensemble's French horn section. They debated whether Dominik Hasek was or wasn't the greatest

Buffalo Sabre of all time. But then, the topic turned to life after high school. To their separate, adult lives. James revealed how badly he freaked out on Janelle's wedding day, unable to fathom her being with someone else. Janelle admitted that she still stalked James on social media, imagining an alternate reality in which they had gotten married and started a family.

Driving in silence, I started to feel like I was eavesdropping. As if I was intruding. At the same time, I found myself intrigued. Interested in my two passengers, even rooting for their relationship, as if it were some real-life version of *The Notebook*. I was emotionally invested. I wanted to see what would happen. How would this chance encounter affect them? Were they going to just part ways, go back to their families, and move on? Or would this conversation re-ignite their feelings and create problems for their current love lives? Would it leave splinters that might fester? But then, we found ourselves pulling up to the airport and I was forced to imagine answers to my questions.

Driving away from the terminal that day, what stuck with me the most was just how unlikely that rendezvous was. The more I thought about it, the more unbelievable it seemed. Of all the people in the world, in all the cities that exist, getting rides to and from all the places in those cities - somehow James and Janelle found each other in my car. It felt like destiny.

Then, as I considered it further, I realized that same spark of fate had been present for every other passenger who had gotten in my car as well. Over three years of driving, I met thousands of people, from at least twenty-seven different countries, speaking dozens of languages, representing all sorts of life experiences. And with each and every passenger, there were millions of decisions and happenings that led to them being in my car. A meeting ran late. Their vehicle was in the shop. The algorithm connected their request to my profile. If one detail had been altered, I never would've met them. We wouldn't have shared those moments.

Of course, it's not just rideshare. Every interaction with anyone is a once-in-a-lifetime experience. An opportunity for lives to intersect. And, when we're open to it, an opportunity for our lives to be changed in minute ways. Or in major ways. Every day we go through dozens of intersections, which hold infinite potential. The chance to learn or unlearn. To feel. To understand. To inspire. The opportunity to let go. To be energized or soothed. To gain perspective.

I didn't always see these intersections that way. It was a conversation with passengers in my car (the last story in this book, actually) that grabbed my attention and opened my eyes, showing me how precious these moments are. How enlightening these intersections could be, when we take advantage. So, I started listening, and asking questions, and paying attention. I collected experiences. I absorbed wisdom. And now, I'm sharing those intersections with you.

"True Fiction"

Every story in this collection is true, based on my real-life interactions with rideshare passengers (I have each rider's permission and I changed certain specifics for their privacy). And yet, each of the stories are also fictitious because I've added narrative structure, created back-stories, invented context, and adjusted details. The basic facts of each story are true to how they were experienced or how they were shared with me, and yet they were infused with my perspective, my assumptions and biases, and even my imagination.

Of course, that's how the "truth" works, most of the time. And in my experience, our hang-ups with which parts of a story are objectively accurate or what details are fabrications end up eclipsing the beauty and wisdom we were meant to see. Like an audience at a magic show, if we insist on being detectives, we end up missing out on wonder.

And so, I'm offering you these nine tales, not as a journalist or fact-recorder, but as a storyteller. I'm inviting you to pause investigation and suspend judgment. To marvel at the people behind the characters. To find the meaning in their humanity. And, if you're looking for it, you might just see the truth in these fictions.

PART 1 - WATER

I'd rather be water than sand
Not a lonely granule, while surrounded on land,
An indistinguishable drop that could not stand
Alone
I'd rather be rolling with others, hand in hand,
Interconnected with an oceanic span.

Water is always plural,
Even a single drop or swirl,
Just like every boy and/or girl,
Because Human is also plural.

Sand only sticks together when water serves as glue.
In fact, water is an agent of transformation for others too.
The waves of togetherness crash through barriers,
Squelch destructive fires, and carve rock's layers.

In the end, water is used to wash off the sand,
Until only liquid is left clinging to each human leg and hand,
Reminding us of our origins off-land,
Exemplifying for us how to band-

Together.

THE JUMPER

Thursday, 7:45am, SODO

I felt the hair on the back of my neck stand up as I pulled up to the pickup location for my next passenger, Ali, and scanned the area for any doors in or out of the warehouse. Something about the building was off. It looked abandoned, with graffiti decorating the exterior and overgrown weeds filling the spaces where trucks should have been loading and unloading. There was no one around. The whole block was an industrial ghost-town.

I pulled closer to the structure, and that's when I saw the few subtle hints of life. Camouflaged to the building, there were a handful of security cameras which looked state of the art. Seeing where a few of them were pointed, I focused my eyes on the corner next to the loading docks, where it jutted out toward the street. There, tucked into the shadows, was a metal door with no handle and some sort of electronic device mounted on the wall next to it. This was not an abandoned warehouse. It was something else disguised as one.

Just as my imagination was getting ready to crank out some wonderfully absurd conspiracy theories about what might be inside, the metal door opened, and Ali slipped out. She was short and thin, dressed in dark blue skinny jeans and a flannel shirt, and the sides of her head were buzzed, leading to a lavender fauxhawk on top, kept in place with gel. She walked the sixty feet to the car with purpose. Short, swift strides. Like a secret agent, or a jewel thief headed for her getaway car, trying not to draw attention to herself. I had so many questions as she yanked the car door open and hopped in the front seat, but she spoke first.

"Hi, sorry," she said with the nervous energy of a first-time skydiver, "I just got off work and a lot of shit happened. I kind of want to tell someone about it, but I don't know who! Could I maybe talk to you about it?"

I was stunned at the way she jumped right in. "Uh, yeah… you can tell me about work. Wait, you work in that building? What is your job?"

Should I check to see if this is even Ali? And am I just assuming that this address in the app, which is thirty minutes away, is where she's headed and just going with it?

She looked at me, considering whether to proceed or not. "Yes, I work in that building. I'm not really supposed to talk about any of this, so please just pretend that you don't hear anything, ok?"

Who cares if this is Ali or not... I really want to hear this!

"Yeah, totally" I said, "You were never here, and I never heard nothing." I mimed zipping my mouth closed and locking it.

"Perfect." Ali took a deep breath. "Ok, so I coordinate on-site building security for TechTron."

"THE TechTron?!?" I interrupted, loudly.

"Right... *the* TechTron," she shot back, indulging me.

"What? That's impressive! But what do you mean you 'coordinate security'?"

"Well, mostly it's just staying in contact with our on-site security personnel, making sure any incidents are being monitored, things like that. I mean, this is TechTron, so we get a fair number of threats and what not."

"Well, sure," I said, smirking, "I mean, who doesn't?! Right?"

She flashed a half-smile and resumed sharing her job description.

"Yeah, so I work over night here, which means all of our buildings in Asia are fully staffed and operational, so I basically keep an eye on employee risks, threats, and any incidents that arise."

"Whoa," I said, trying to muffle how impressed I was. "You do all of that from *that* building?" I said, pointing behind us. "I mean, I'm not saying you're lying, but that just looked like an old, abandoned warehouse to me."

"Right. That's on purpose. It's sort of a secret location. Every ten weeks or so, our office moves to a new building, always trying to blend in, I guess. We've only been in that warehouse for about a week now. We were in an old grocery store before."

"Wait a second… So, every ten weeks, you have to move?"

"Yeah, but it's no big deal. I don't do anything. The facility team will scout locations and get our next one ready to roll. Then, two nights ahead of the move, I'll get the address and I just show up on the day to some random building and it's our new office."

"That's so fascinating," I said, "like some spy movie with CIA black sites and safe houses or something."

"Yeah, I guess it is a bit unusual," she responded, considering how this all might sound to an outsider, "but I'm used to it."

We had only driven a half-mile by this point, and she was anxious to tell me what had happened during the night.

"OK, so can I tell you about the incident last night?"

"Of course, sorry," I said, trying to contain myself. For some reason she was trusting me with this top-secret story, and I didn't want to ruin my opportunity.

8 Hours Earlier
Thursday, 3:00pm local time, Shanghai, China

Jian sat in her chair, staring at the blinking cursor on her computer screen. The blank page was one final bully reinforcing her inadequacy. Her mind was screaming.

You never get anything right! You're a total screw up. Look! You can't even write your own suicide note...

This feeling never left her. Her coworker all day and companion all night. But not "getting it right" was only one part of it. It wasn't just that she was inadequate. It was that whatever she was - her essence or personality or true self - was wrong. She didn't belong. Unacceptable. She didn't have enough good qualities, and the qualities she had the most of were the bad ones. Jian had felt this way for most of her life.

Some of Jian's earliest memories were of others teasing her. She had always fit in better with the young boys and found herself wanting to play "boy games," while all her female peers would hide their snickers with their hands. No matter how hard she tried, Jian could never sit still, stay quiet, and act submissive, like a traditional Chinese girl was supposed to. She couldn't help it. She had the fighting spirit of a jaguar and the boundless energy of a hummingbird. But the teasing laughter of grade-school girls was just a mild introduction to the harassment that would follow in the coming years.

As Jian went through puberty, new differences emerged. She was definitely attracted to girls, rather than boys, and that was a scary reality. Even though public opinion had come a long way, she was well aware of how horrible life had been for anyone bucking the traditional systems throughout her country's history. She was even more keenly aware of how much this news would confuse and anger her parents.

While most of her friends at school might react to her coming out with curiosity or jealousy, seeing her sexuality as a mystifying badge for their token collections, her parents would be embarrassed of her, and the ensuing shame would be unbearable. So, Jian avoided the topic of sexuality at all costs, and, to her delight, her parents followed suit.

But eventually, Jian's anxiety started to shift. By the time Jian was graduating high school, what she used to think of as her personal style choices - shorter hair, athletic clothes, and a chiseled body - had become something closer to her identity. She didn't think about her career possibilities, or who she wanted to make out with. Jian was obsessed with the idea that she was still not fully formed - still coming to terms with who she was or could be. And how that person fit in with or stuck out from the people around her.

And so, she lived in pursuit of her true self. As she cut her hair even shorter and shopped exclusively in the boys clothing section, she crossed over some invisible threshold. A point of no return.

At her university, everyone Jian would meet just assumed she was queer, but now the curiosity was missing. Gone were the raised eyebrows and smirking lips when someone popped the question. In fact, people were no longer even asking at all. Was it possible that she was disappointing her straight friends by not being the "right kind of lesbian?"

Every day her ears would be pelted with heart-numbing filth. Complete strangers' smiles would shift into scowls when they got close enough to realize she wasn't a man, and then they'd call her a "psycho" or "dyke" or "tranny" or "cunt" or "dickgirl" or "hun dan" ("mixed egg" or "bastard").

One night during her second year, Jian was walking back to her dorm after having spent the evening sipping tea and reading an enthralling fantasy sci-fi thriller set in another galaxy, when a group of students started harassing her. Five or six unathletic boys, taking out their insecurities on her, verbally vomiting the usual tropes and bigotry.

"Nice outfit... for a dude. If you weren't trying so hard to look like a man, people might like you!"

"Yeah, with the right outfit you could be sexy!"

"By the right outfit, he means naked."

They all laughed at her and simultaneously imagined her without clothes.

"Nah, don't listen to them. You just need to smile more! With a smile you'd be so much more attractive!"

"Yeah, you might even look like a woman!"

"Eh, she's pretty enough for you already... What do you think? You wanna get with him?"

The group of harassers walked alongside Jian, even as she picked up her pace. They started pushing and shoving her, trying to evoke a reaction.

"What's the matter?"

"Yeah, do you need a man to walk you home?"

"To protect you?!"

"To keep you safe?!"

"No, I think she's too rebellious for that."
"That's right. She needs to be taught a lesson!"
"My dick is a good teacher!"

At first, they just laughed at their own suggestions of rape. But, as soon as Jian reacted, everything escalated. She told them to stop so they grabbed her arm and led her across the street. She yelled for help, but her resistance fueled them. Two of them pinned her against a parked car. Right under a streetlight, exposed for anyone to see. She screamed her dissent. One of them violently yanked her shorts to her ankles. Her brain blacked out the rest.

Her next memory was from the following morning. Waking up, telling herself it was just a nightmare. That she wouldn't give it another thought ever again. That she'd never tell anyone.

So, Jian felt more and more isolated as her college days wore on. Frequent night terrors reliving that fateful night or panic attacks when she saw someone on the street that resembled one of her attackers. Rearranging her life to avoid vulnerable situations. Keeping her distance from everyone, including roommates and friends, as she continued trying to figure herself out.

Her peers kept making their assumptions about her sexuality, but Jian began to worry about new questions. She was still very young, and unsure about her sexuality in some ways. What if it turned out that she *was* into men in the end? How could she be with a man sexually after experiencing such debilitating trauma? How could she be with *anyone* sexually when she can't even see her own naked body in the bathroom mirror without nausea? Would there be a place in society for someone who was asexual?

By her final year of college, Jian had become a hermit. Her quest to find her true self had left her confused, exhausted, and angry. She hated feeling so alone, but every minute with other people was a torturous combination of fear and self-hatred. It all came down, it seemed, to two options: commit suicide or live the remaining four months of college based on one rule: do whatever the hell you want without any concern for who her "true self" was.

She chose the second option, and to reward herself for continuing to live, Jian shaved her head, got a tattoo across her chest that said "Ren de" ("Human"), and ordered a new pair of Air Jordans. But even as she felt a new sense of freedom, the desire to tell someone - to share her traumatic story, to explain who she had become, to vent out all the worry and angst - nagged at her. She had struggled through every stage of her life alone, and it was that sense of loneliness she couldn't shake. She had to let off some steam. Some grief. Some pain. So, she packed a runaway bag just in case, then sat on her dorm room bed to make the hardest phone call of her life. Having no one else to turn to, she dialed her parents' home number.

As Jian sat at her desk in Shanghai, trying desperately to get one thing right before she left this world, her mind found its way back to that phone call, now almost two years ago, though it seemed like decades more. Her father had come to the phone first that day, perhaps sensing that Jian needed him. Remembering his calm, smooth voice caused Jian to weep, and as her tears started falling onto her keyboard she wondered if they might be able to type the letter for her. During that call, her dad had told Jian that he'd known she was different since the moment she was born. That he would always love her, no matter what. That he would be there for her whenever she needed him.

Back then, her parents' acceptance had soothed her pain, but Jian saw now that it had also sowed the seed of a new demonic vine. After all, what sort of monster assumes the worst about their own parents and expects them to reject their child? What kind of daughter had she been, hiding core truths about herself and depriving her parents of the opportunity to show love and support? By villainizing her parents all those years, she had found herself to be the true enemy.

Over the twenty months since the phone call, Jian's vine grew and grew, wrapping itself around every facet of her life. Every memory from her past. As she encountered each new cyber-bully, the vine would squeeze tighter. The words would prick and sting as she read them, but their trolling hostility paled in comparison to the venom of her own self-disdain. Every step along her miserable life had brought her closer to finding her true self. And that was the problem. It was clear now:

She was the common denominator in all the heartache.

Her temperament at age six. Her middle school grades. Her sexuality, and eventually, her lack thereof. Her style. Her choices for college and for her career. Her lack of financial success. Her treatment of her parents. Her inability to fit into traditional stereotypes. Her addiction to reading every mean text, social media troll, and slur-lined email over and over again. The massive ice block of shame that kept her from second dates, second therapy visits, or ever talking with anyone about almost anything serious. Her nightly ritual - using a razor blade on her forearms, so she didn't have to feel the emotional pain. And to punish herself for being the problem. It was penance. After all, there's no forgiveness for sins without the shedding of blood.

The problem at every turn was her - the true self that she'd been obsessed with finding- and it had to be stopped. Her fingers jumped into their harmonious rhythm, producing a one-paragraph symphony to accompany her death. It read:

To anyone who cares,

I am a virus. A glitch. An anomaly that does not have a place here. In order to spare all of you from having to see, hear, or otherwise interact with me, I'm being permanently deleted. Though it's too late for me, I do hope that the next person like me will find themselves to be good enough for this world.

She added her team members' emails to the recipients' box, along with a few select higher-ups who had unleashed their slurs or salacious gossip at some point; but, as her hand led the mouse pointer to the send button, her pointer finger froze. Images of her mother identifying her body on the pavement, and of her father spreading her ashes in the East

China Sea hijacked her focus. She had expected this, of course, knowing that her biological self would go to war in order to keep her alive. In fact, she had planned for it.

Jian had set up a scheduled email to her parents, a few relatives, and the only two people she considered friends. That email didn't rely on her ability to wrangle her lesser-evolved self to click any buttons or pull any levers - it was already in motion, with a failsafe mechanism that made it unable to be canceled. The finality of that scheduled letter steeled her nerves, and she clicked send.

"I guess this is happening," she said out-loud to herself slowly, trying to ignore the fact that her hands were shaking. "Still, no harm in having a snack first."

She locked her workstation and headed down the hall to the secure area where her phone was stored. After passing through the two sets of double doors, she swiped her badge on the reader at waist level. A postcard-sized, red metal door with "F9" painted on it swung open near her ankles. She reached inside, grabbed her phone and ear buds, slammed the locker shut, and headed down to the cafeteria.

She hadn't even unlocked the phone yet, but she could see three notifications. Two texts and one Instagram direct message. She swiped her index finger across the screen and tapped the six-digit password to unlock her phone so she could read today's hate-mail. All three messages were full of venomous sexism and homophobia. Icing on her suicide-cake. Jian shrugged her shoulders at these wasted efforts. Three soldiers still firing bullets after the white flag had been raised.

Grabbing a blueberry muffin from the a la carte cafe, Jian performed a mental-walk-through of the next several hours. What would be the last few hours of her life plus the small amount of chaos her death might cause. She paused when she pictured her mom and dad receiving the news. It wasn't their pain that worried her - Jian didn't want them to suffer the heartbreak but knew that was a necessary evil. She was more concerned about whether they would understand. Whether they would know why their child decided to die.

She wondered if she had included enough context in the scheduled email to her parents. She thought back, trying to remember the details of the email she had written the day before, but she couldn't summon the actual words. Only the finality of it all. The surety that the message would be delivered and that her parents would know *what* happened. But would they know *why?* Just to be sure, Jian decided to forward a few of her recent text conversations to her mom. She added an accompanying note: "I just want it to end."

Thursday, 1:15am, SODO
(5:15pm in Shanghai, China)

"Ali, we've got an incoming from the on-site at Building 131, Shanghai."

Ali looked up from the report she was scanning and took in the details laid out on the screen in front of her.

"Interpreter?" She asked. Her coworker sitting a few yards to her left flashed a thumbs-up sign over his head without turning around. She glanced down to check the time in

Shanghai, then tapped the flashing green button on her screen, connecting the call to her headset.

"Good afternoon, this is Ali, #491277. Who am I speaking with?"

Ali waited for the on-site's mandarin sentence to finish and the interpreter to repeat it back to her.

"Yes, this is Li, #884901 at building 131, with a code yellow."

A code yellow situation was almost always nothing to worry about, except for those doing the paperwork. It involved doing a wellness check on an employee and it could be triggered by any number of situations. Maybe someone decided to work from home for a while and that was out of pattern for them. Perhaps someone thought a co-worker was acting strange, and anonymously requested a wellness check. And every once in a while, like today, a wellness check would be triggered by a concerned family member calling the company.

Ali tapped the check mark next to the Employee ID on her screen, letting the system know that she had verified him, exhaled, and then responded.

"Thanks for verifying Li. What's the situation?"

Through the interpreter on the line, Li informed Ali that he had a wellness check request from the mother of an employee named Jian, and that her mother was still on hold, demanding to be connected to her daughter. Li had called Ali first, as was standard procedure, so Ali and her team could determine if this was a credible request, and if a wellness check was warranted. Ali would now transform into the judge, and her team of jurors would pour over the facts of the case for about two minutes, before reaching a verdict: check or no check.

Ali went through the basic questions to gather information. The Situation Report form had been activated by one of Ali's team members and was filling the large fifty-five-inch monitor in the center of their command center. The AI-powered software was filling in each section, pulling from Ali's words. It had been designed to only pull the relevant information and input it into a one-page report, but in order to err on the safe side, the settings basically turned it into a conversation-transcriber. After a few edits by Ali's right-hand man Tre, the screen displayed a summary of the situation.

Reason for Wellness Check Request: Her mother thinks she's suicidal, because of the texts she sent her a few hours ago.

Any Relevant Employee HR Notes: Average Performance Reviews, no previous reports

Most Recent Badge Swipe: Building 131, Floor 8, South

Real-time Badge Tracking: Yes

Most Recent Self-Health Evaluation: 5 - Excellent

Ali's eyes darted back and forth between the sections of the report. Her team was doing the same. Everyone knew that this case was headed toward a verdict of "no check." You needed more than just a family member's concern to disrupt someone's day and subject them to a series of interview questions which assume they might want to harm themselves or commit suicide.

Still, something wasn't sitting right in Ali's stomach. She wanted to know what was said in those text messages.

"Can I talk to her mother?" she asked Li through the interpreter. She waited a few seconds and heard nothing, so she tried again.

"Is she still on hold? I want to speak with her."

"Um... I guess so?! Is that against the rules?"

Li's question was genuine. He had been on the job for a mere ten days and this was only his second code yellow. The first code yellow was a few days prior. A system-generated code, based on an employee not reporting back in after a scheduled vacation had ended (they had taken another job without telling TechTron, wondering how long they would still get a paycheck if no one noticed). But even if Li had been a veteran TechTron On-Site, he wouldn't have known if he was allowed to connect an employee's family member to the TechTron Security Coordinator, who was housed five-thousand, seven-hundred miles away. Most family members didn't demand action like Jian's mother, and they certainly didn't wait on hold expecting to talk to the employee like this. Despite having six years on the job and working through hundreds of code yellows, this was the first time Ali had ever requested this.

"I don't think it's a problem, but I'll make sure the report shows that I requested this," Ali said. Even without being a mother herself, Ali could sense the desperation that Jian's mom must've been feeling to come across this strongly.

After a few seconds, Li connected Ali and her interpreter to Jian's mom.

Jian's mom was already halfway through her first sentence. Ali couldn't understand her but heard the name "Jian" a few times. She didn't wait for the interpreter before jumping in.

"Hello, this is Ali. I work for TechTron Security and I'm using an interpreter to speak with you. I want to talk to you and make sure we are keeping Jian safe." She hoped the interpreter could convey her warm, authentic tone in Mandarin.

"I want to speak with Jian. I need to talk to her now." Jian's mother sounded even more desperate than Ali had expected. She started to feel like a hostage negotiator and wondered if she had made a mistake trying to talk to this woman.

"I understand. I will try to work on that." Ali put her palm to her forehead and shook her head as the translator repeated her. "Li said that Jian was texting you today. What did she say?"

Jian's mother exploded with phrase after phrase and Ali was sure the interpreter would forget half of what she was saying. When she finally stopped long enough for the interpreter to start in, Ali had already adjusted her computer's software, making sure every word would be transcribed.

It took four and a half minutes before Ali could get another sentence in, as Jian's mother shared the all too familiar story of cyber-bullying. Ali put the phone call on hold for a minute to discuss it with her team. She relied on her team in moments like this and listened carefully to each one as they shared. Every jury member had their own opinion.

"She sounds like an over-protective mom to me. I don't think we have a credible threat."

"Over-protective? Sure, but also some of those texts were brutal. I get why she's concerned."

"Yeah, and bullying like this is no joke."

"Ok, ok. But the real question is this - Are our asses covered if we don't do a wellness check? That's our process, right? If we go 'no-check,' are we exposed to litigation risks?"

Heads nodded in agreement that this was the crux of the matter, and some heads shook trying to answer the question.

"No, we're good either way here."

"Agreed."

"Ali - it's up to you," Tre summarized, "no risk, but we can also make the case that there's enough there for a check."

"Maybe," came the dissenting final word.

Ali took Jian's mother off hold and shared the battle plan. They would not do a wellness check yet, but they would keep two team members watching Jian's every movement for the next few hours, while the On-Site would go get a visual check on Jian every hour until she left the office (typically around 8:00pm). And as for talking to Jian on the phone, she'd have to wait until Jian left the secure area of the building and retrieved her phone from the holding area like normal. Ali didn't want Jian to know they were coordinating with her mom behind her back. Ali also agreed to check-in calls with Jian's mother every ninety minutes, that way the team could update her if needed, and she could share any new information that came to light. Everyone agreed that this was a workable compromise, including Jian's mom.

Thursday, 6:00pm local time, Shanghai, China

Li was happy to have a little excitement to his job for once. Every one of the ten days working at Building #131 so far had been a yawner. He'd spent each shift sitting next to the metal detectors and turnstiles, watching the hordes of employees swiping their badges, and occasionally closing a stuck stairwell door or investigating a conference room that had unscheduled occupants. During training, Li had gotten excited about perimeter checks, threat analysis, and digital defenses - all things that made him feel like he was joining a military spy unit, not babysitting motion sensors.

This was his first real code yellow, and he was ready to have something to do, even if it was just to go look at an employee. What, exactly, was he supposed to be looking for? Could you tell if someone was intending to harm themselves just by staring at them while they work? Was she going to be sharpening a knife or something? The manual mostly described how to read facial expressions to see if someone was upset, but Li felt very uncomfortable drawing any conclusions based on someone being angry. After all, if a bothered face was an indication of threat, then Li would have to file reports on about twenty-five percent of employees passing by his station every morning.

But either way, Li knew he had about fifteen minutes until his check-in with Ali and he needed to get a visual check on Jian. He locked his station and walked toward the elevators to head to the eighth floor.

Andrew Spink

Building 131 was a dark glass skyscraper, right in the center of Shanghai's sea of concrete. It was a perfect rectangular prism for the first fifteen floors, before narrowing to allow for open-air rooftop decks, which alternated sides of the building every eight or nine stories. In theory, employees would be able to relax in the fresh air, or even have meetings out there, but the air pollution made sure the decks were empty most of the time. There were sixty stories in all. TechTron occupied forty, and from what Li had heard, the top twenty floors were filled with over-priced, closet-sized hotel rooms.

From Li's desk just inside the main security checkpoint, he could see all three public building entrances. No matter which door you entered, you'd be funneled by glass walls to the four metal detectors, badge scanners, and various other hidden sensors that made up the first line of defense. From there, you had options. The main lobby opened into a massive lounge, with a high vaulted ceiling and several couches imitating penthouse living rooms. There were standing desk workstations, floor cushions, and hammock chairs spread around. The back half of the room had a lofted cafeteria above it, accessed by the escalators that flanked the elevator banks in the center. It was stunning to look at, as long as it wasn't during the morning or afternoon logjam of employees all trying to move through the six elevators, squeeze past the security checkpoint, and get through the doors.

Li swiped his badge across one of the touch screens situated ten feet in front of the entrance to the elevators and tapped the number eight. The screen refreshed to an overhead layout of the elevator banks, highlighting the second car on the left, which had just opened its doors and illuminated the small round light above the opened doors with the same shade of blue that the screen had shown Li. He stepped inside the button-less chamber warily. He was still getting used to trusting technology at this level - a "must" when you work for TechTron.

Stepping off the elevator onto the eighth floor, Li paused and pulled out his phone to check Jian's file. Her last badge scan was at the door right in front of him, over two hours ago, so she was on the eighth floor. He scrolled down to see her workstation's location, as he swiped his badge and passed through the glass doors separating the south work areas from the elevators.

The floor was nearly empty, as normal. Most people at TechTron worked from home at least half of the time, only coming into the office for meetings or to take advantage of the top-notch food, massages, and fitness center.

Every floor, in every TechTron building, had the same general blueprint and was set up the same way. Elevator banks in the center, with north and south doors isolating them from the desks. Like an equator, conference rooms formed a barrier between halves, with a few pass-through points, and a kitchenette was set up against the elevator walls on one side, with bathrooms on the other. This was to make things more efficient if you were heading to a different floor or building for a meeting, or switching teams, but for Li it just made things more difficult. He was never really sure exactly where he was. There were no landmarks.

Jian's desk was in the southwest quadrant, all the way against the west-facing windows. Li double checked his phone as he approached her workstation. He was so worried about getting the right desk that he didn't realize the entire quadrant was empty until he was standing at Jian's workstation.

There was a trace of worry rising in his stomach as he spun around and scanned as much of the floor as he could see. There was no sign of Jian anywhere. Her desk looked untouched. He knew he should have checked on her earlier. Every second he stood there, dumbfounded, he grew more concerned.

He reassured himself by thinking of all the places she could be, other than at her workstation. He could see a group of people in one of the conference rooms across the way, so he moved closer to get a better look. The blurry mass sharpened into four distinct people, none of which resembled the picture Li kept compulsively checking on his phone.

"Great! I'm too late." he thought, starting to imagine all the ways Jian could've already committed suicide. The windows didn't open on this floor, so the only options he could think of were hanging or stabbing. Either would be difficult, considering this was a secure floor, with very limited access to even basic office equipment.

"Do you need something?" The man's voice surprised Li, who realized he had been standing just outside the conference room, still staring.

"Oh my God, I'm so sorry," Li said, not answering his question. He hadn't prepared for this scenario. He'd thought of everything except that there might be other people on the floor, and that they might ask him what he was doing. How would he explain this?

"I'm just… I am lost." The words escaped before he could stop them. "I'm new to this building, just started last week or so."

"Ok, well this is floor eight - one of the secure floors. I'm not sure you're supposed to be up here. What are you looking for?"

Li mumbled a few things about quadrants and needing a compass to get around and backed away toward the elevators. He had escaped unscathed, but every second he spent on floor eight without seeing Jian inched him closer to a panic attack.

"Maybe she drafted off someone else's badge swipe and slipped to a different floor," he thought to himself before remembering how TechTron's smart elevators had sensors monitoring everything, including the number of people in the elevator car and overall weight. If there was an extra body somewhere, he would have already seen the irregularity report. Unless she had stolen a badge off someone with a similar build, she had to be on this floor, but where?

Li gave up his search efforts and decided to head back to his desk and call Ali. He headed past the central block of restrooms, sidestepping to avoid collision with the woman coming out of the all-gender single-stall bathroom, and turned the corner, swiping his badge and pushing "L" on the touch screen.

It wasn't until he stepped into the elevator car that the face of the woman he just sidestepped registered in his consciousness. It was Jian. Relief overtook him. She was alive! But Li knew he'd have to report on more than whether Jian was alive or not. He tried to stabilize his breathing and recall her face. Was she upset? Did she look like she was a danger to herself or others? Everything was a blur. Somehow, he was confident that woman was Jian, but nothing more.

He convinced himself that she was fine, reaching for his phone to begin the report. It was already ringing, and he recognized the phone number from earlier as Jian's mother.

Thursday, 2:10am, SODO
(6:10pm in Shanghai, China)

Ali checked the time as she slipped her headset back on. Only an hour or two until Jian would be going home for the evening, when they could all file the code yellow away with the others and move on. She knew her choice to monitor Jian's situation had placed an extra burden on her team, who also had to continue their regular duties all night. In the last hour alone, there were four other incidents called in, all accompanied by paperwork. Ali made a mental note to find a way to reward them after this was over. For now, it was time for another check-in. She made eye-contact with all three members of her team, receiving head nods in return, then tapped her screen, sending the incoming call to the room's speakers.

"This is Ali, #491277. Who am I speaking with?"

"Hi Ali, Li, #884901 at building 131." Li didn't wait for the interpreter to finish before continuing. "I just did a visual check on Jian, and she seemed fine, but her mom is on the phone again and she's out of control."

"Ok, we can deal with her mom in a minute. How long ago was your visual check?"

"I just did it," Li said, "about five minutes ago."

"And how did she seem?"

"She was fine, I think, but her mom is really upset. She wants to talk to you."

Ali was not about to allow an upset mother to dictate the situation. "Tell her I'll talk to her in thirty minutes when I promised to check in with her."

Li spoke so fast the interpreter could barely keep up. "I did tell her that. I told her at least three times. But she saw an email from Jian that made her really upset and she won't listen to me. She wants me to go back up and check on Jian again."

"Ok, ok," Ali responded, trying to calm Li down, "What is this email you're talking about?"

"I don't know. She wouldn't listen to me. I was trying to tell her I just checked on her, but she kept saying that Jian was dead."

This was sounding weirder by the second. Ali muted herself and checked with her team. There were no emails sent from Jian's account to external recipients, so they did not have any info about the email. They did, however, uncover the one email she'd sent today. It was to some fellow employees.

"Put it on center screen, please," Ali said. And with the click of a button, the room froze. Everyone stared at the words, translated into English by the system:

"I am a virus. A glitch. An anomaly that does not have a place here. In order to spare all of you from having to see, hear, or otherwise interact with me, I'm being permanently deleted. Though it's too late for me, I do hope that the next person like me will find themselves to be good enough for this world."

The seriousness of the situation washed over Ali like an unexpected wave at the beach, knocking her off balance. She collapsed into her chair, trying to figure out what to do. This was the furthest a code yellow had ever gone. There was always a moment when they realized it was a false alarm. She couldn't even remember what she was supposed to do if they decided someone was truly a threat. Ali clicked back into her call.

"Li, can you patch her mom through? I want to hear more about the email she received."

For the first few exchanges, Ali was just trying to get Jian's mother to slow down and complete a sentence. The email had obviously been extremely upsetting. The fragments that Ali was able to piece together through the translator made her breath catch. It was another suicide note. Her fingernails dug into the armrests on her chair. She needed Li to go back to the eighth floor immediately. She put Jian's mom on hold and switched over to Li, but before she could say anything she was cut off by one of her team members, yelling out in panic.

"Jian's on the move!"

Jian's email slid to the left as the center of the three monitors in front of Ali started tracking Jian's movement. Large red letters spelled out "Bldg 131, 8th Floor Elevators" in the middle box on the screen, which was labeled "Most Recent Badge Scan."

Ali's voice shook as she cried out, "Is she going up or down?" There was no answer.

"UP OR DOWN?!" She yelled more urgently.

"We don't know!" came the reply. Their system only reported badge swipes, not the other, normally irrelevant data Ali craved in this moment.

"Li - get ready to run to the elevators. Jian's moving."

Li responded with the tone of a veteran soldier receiving his orders. "Got it. What floor?"

"I don't know yet," Ali said softly, staring at the screen.

After what seemed like hours, the text rearranged itself to say "Bldg 131, 24th Floor North."

Ali needed more information. "What's on the twenty-fourth floor?" she demanded. Her team clicked and tapped on their computers, searching for clues.

"Pulling up the floorplan now... Nothing, it's just another floor. Same as all the rest."

"Is it possible she's heading to a meeting?"

"Unlikely. She has nothing scheduled."

Ali knew they couldn't waste precious seconds debating her motives for choosing this floor.

"Ali!"

"I see it," she acknowledged, before re-centering her headset's microphone.

"Li! Twenty-fourth floor now!" she demanded.

They had found the missing piece. The twenty-fourth floor had an open-air deck on the north side. Jian was going to jump.

Thursday, 6:27pm local time, Shanghai, China

Li

Li sprinted to the lobby elevators, holding his badge out, ready to swipe. Something had clicked into place and he no longer felt anything besides the urgency of this moment. Gone was the excitement over finally seeing some action. The concern about getting things right and not feeling awkward had vanished. All that mattered was Jian.

Li pushed the touch screen, selecting the twenty-fourth floor and watched impatiently for directions. Ali was asking him something in his earpiece and he waited for the interpreter to relay it as he rushed into the open elevator car.

"Is it possible to broadcast a message over the building speakers?" Ali's question caught Li by surprise, and at first, he didn't make the connection. There was an emergency broadcast function embedded within his security app, in case there was a major security threat, like a gunman or a bomb threat. In training, they had joked about the broadcast system being for a zombie apocalypse.

"I think so, yeah." He tried to find the function on his phone.

Following Ali's instructions, Li sent a broadcast building-wide, while stepping out of the elevator and swiping his badge on the twenty-fourth floor's north doors. There was something sobering about hearing his own voice crackling through the ceiling.

"Jian Zhang, please check in with security. Your mother is on the phone."

Li reached the doors leading to the deck. He could see Jian standing on a chair she had pulled over to the railing. He paused with his hand on the door handle, begging for the universe to wake him from this nightmare.

Jian

Moving through the twenty-fourth floor, Jian felt like her insides were going to explode. She couldn't keep the reality of what was about to happen from spreading throughout her consciousness. Each step closer to the deck doors was a miniature war to be won. She knew she couldn't stop. Hesitation would open a window of opportunity for her survival instincts to rise up. She couldn't afford a coup. Her email had gone out and her parents would see it soon enough. This was going to happen, and she wasn't going to let anything stop her.

The open-air deck ran the full width of the building, with a three-and-a-half-foot tall glass railing lining the outer edge. There were a handful of people scattered around the workstations that filled the north half of the floor, so she would have to be careful. Slipping out the center doors, she scanned the deck. It was an empty span of cafe tables, chairs, hammocks, and short potted plants. Every inch of the outer railing was visible from inside.

Jian's internal resistance was strengthening, now that she could feel the wind on her face. Now that she could see the future crime scene. She plodded on, putting one foot in front of the other, moving slowly toward the center of the north edge. She had chosen this spot carefully. She was high enough up to avoid any concern about surviving the fall, but low enough that the scene on the pavement below would be as minimal as possible. The north side of the building was the only one without an entrance - pedestrian or garage, so no TechTron employees would have their commute impacted. She wanted her death to be as little a distraction as possible.

Trying to steady her hands, Jian slid one of the chairs toward the railing, the scraping of the chair's legs on the concrete making her flinch. When she finally convinced her body to step up onto the chair, a gust of wind caught her by surprise, and she faltered. Her left leg instinctively took a steadying step back, off the edge of the chair, and her shin smacked the corner, drawing blood. The pain was sharp, and out of weariness, Jian doubled over. Tears breached her eyelets and rolled down her cheeks. She wasn't sure if she was crying because of the pain, the tiredness, or the difficulty of what she was trying to do. This, the most onerous task she had ever faced, was also the loneliest. No one was with her. No one was cheering her on as she overcame each internal battle. No one was witnessing her fortitude. The strength she had to drum up. It was just her.

Taking a deep breath, she steadied herself, limped back onto the chair, and took a peek over the edge. The vertigo was debilitating, and she grabbed the railing for support, when she heard a voice from the speakers behind her.

"Jian Zhang, please check in with security. Your mother is on the phone."

The surprise of hearing her own name over the building speakers almost sent her over the edge by accident. What was going on? Why was her mother on the phone? How was her mom capable of getting through to her building, and having someone broadcast this message? Did she somehow know what was happening? She thought of the email she wrote. It went out minutes ago, but she assumed her mother wouldn't read that for hours, if not days.

One hand at a time, Jian transferred her steadying grip from the railing to the back of the chair, crouched down, and turned around to face the building. Her leg was throbbing, and the tears were blurring her vision, but she could make out a man in a security outfit standing just outside the deck doors, holding his phone out next to his head, panic all over his face.

Ali

Any concern about what the procedures were had been thrown out the window, even though Ali was usually a by-the-book sort of person. In fact, normally, Ali was the one who had written the book. But, sooner or later, all the theory and procedures get lost in the face of reality. A real person was trying to end her own life, and Ali knew she could save her. That she had to.

Li broadcasting the message would only buy them a few seconds. She needed the next step to go just right.

"Li," She began, "where are you?"

"Twenty-fourth Floor, almost to the deck," Li said. "I can see Jian on a chair by the edge."

"Ok, listen Li, I'm going to bring Jian's mom back into our call. Are you able to put us on speaker phone?"

"Yea, I can put you on speaker, but…" Li's pause indicated he was taking in the gravity of the situation, and the role he was going to play in it. "Ali…? What do I do?"

Ali knew she didn't have time to prepare Li for this. She couldn't equip any of them for this, even if she had years to do it. They had to act, prepared or not. Every second mattered, and they were working through interpreters.

"It's ok, Li. We're going to save her." She mustered up every remaining particle of confidence. "Just stay calm, move carefully, and follow my instructions."

Li

Li wanted so badly to be anywhere other than on this deck, caught up in this situation. This job was supposed to be mindless and boring. Why couldn't he have been ok with that, instead of going and wishing for some more action?! He was way out of his depth. Every thought of saving Jian was chased away by the fear that he would cause her to jump - that he'd be responsible for her death. He braced himself, twisted the handle to the deck door, and slipped outside to put Ali's plan into action.

He looked at Jian who was staring back at him, without making eye contact. She was almost sitting on the chair, hugging her knees with her right arm and holding onto the chair with her left. He could see a blood stain on her jeans that looked fresh, and she was crying hard.

Even with his phone volume up, there was no way Jian was going to hear her mother's voice over the wind. He needed to get closer. As he took a few steps toward her, Jian

42

scrambled back to her feet, as if to get further away from him. Li froze and held the phone out as far as he could, afraid to move or speak.

"Don't," she shouted. "Get away from me!"

He could hear Jian's mother yelling her name through his phone's speaker, but if Jian could hear it, she didn't show it.

"I have your mom on the phone," he stuttered, "She wants to talk to you."

"No. No… no." Li couldn't tell if Jian was saying no to the phone call, or to him, or to herself.

"Can you hear her?"

Jian didn't answer. Her eyes kept oscillating between the phone, her feet, and the street twenty-four stories below. Li inched closer and closer without any sudden movement.

"Here. You can take the phone if you want."

Jian's mom yelled even louder.

"Jian! Jian! It's mom. Jian! I love you. Please talk to me."

"You're not supposed to be here," Jian said in Li's direction. "You weren't supposed to find out until later."

Li realized she was talking to her mom. He took another step closer.

"Jian!" Her mom shouted. "I'm so sorry. I'm so sorry. Please talk to me."

"I can't mom…. I can't."

Jian's mother was frantic. "Yes, you can! Take the phone. Please."

"I can't take it anymore, mom. I don't belong." Five eternal seconds of silence went by before Jian continued. "Everything hurts and… …and I'm tired." She seemed to be talking at Li now. "I didn't want it to go like this. She shouldn't be here!"

Li was searching for an indication that she might come back down from the chair. She was almost sitting on the railing, still facing Li and the building, holding the railing behind her with one hand and the chair with the other. There was only twelve feet between them now.

Jian's chest expanded as she took in a deep breath and forcefully exhaled it out her nostrils. Li wasn't sure how to interpret anything until he saw her feet start to turn around, carefully. Both hands were on the railing now and she was slowly raising her body higher. This was it. Li knew she was getting ready to jump.

Jian turned her head a quarter turn to the left so she could see Li in her peripheral vision.

"Goodbye," she said to Li. To the phone. To TechTron. To everything.

Li dropped the phone on the pavement as Jian turned her gaze back toward the street below and her leg muscles tightened, ready to pounce.

It was now or never.

He closed the twelve-foot gap and lunged forward just as she started her jump. The three middle fingers on his right hand closed around her waistband, and he held on for dear life. The force or her jump pulled Li right up to the chair, leaving Jian's arms and torso dangling over the edge. Her feet searched for footing, while Li reached over the railing with his left arm and lifted her back onto the chair.

She pulled back somewhat willingly and collapsed into the chair, shaking and sobbing.

Thursday, 6:39pm local time, Shanghai, China

Li picked up the crackling phone from the deck floor and handed it to Jian, who came down and sat on the concrete silently crying, listening to her mom's voice. After a few minutes, Jian handed the phone back to Li and stood up, still wincing from the shin pain. Still breathing fast from the events of the last several minutes. They looked at each other in stunned silence, unsure of what they were supposed to do next. No one even looked up from their desk as Li walked her back through the doors and to the elevators. Either they hadn't seen, or they didn't care. They swiped their badges and Li pushed "L" on the touch pad.

He felt a sense of pride as they rode down in the elevator, and gratitude for Ali's quick action and poise. They had just averted disaster in spectacular fashion, yet almost no one would know about it. An unspoken bond between him and a Security Coordinator on the other side of the world. They walked out of the elevators into the lobby, and Li led them to a couple of armchairs set off by themselves, away from the foot traffic. Jian spoke first.

"Thank you... ...for... ...you know... ...uh, stopping me."

Li gave a slight smile of acknowledgment. "I'm sorry if I hurt you."

"No, I'm fine." Jian knew that the few scrapes and bruises she received wouldn't matter.

While some new shame was beginning to form, she was surprised to find that she mostly felt relief. She had proved her strength to herself. Proved her courage by seeing it through to the end. She had jumped! And yet, she had survived, and she was grateful to be alive. Of course, the pains and heartache of life would still be there, and the next few months would be a gauntlet of self-reflection, increased monitoring, and counseling. But something in that moment, hanging over death's crevice, had re-ignited her resolve. Someone had seen her at her lowest, and decided her life was valuable enough to save.

And so, as she sat in the lobby, waiting for her mother to come pick her up, Jian started weeping again. The tears were a mixture of things that she'd cried over thousands of times - anger, exhaustion, sadness. But this time, there was more, because for the first time in a long time, Jian wasn't alone. For the first time in a long time, she felt the slightest tinge of hope.

HIJACKED

August 10th, 2018 - 8:00pm

It wasn't a typical August night, despite the warm temperature, clear skies, and smell of BBQ in the air. It wasn't typical to have Pearl Jam performing in front of fifty-thousand fans, in their hometown for the first time in five years. Pearl Jam fans are not typical fans. They flock to concert venues from all over the world (the longer the distance traveled, the bigger the badge of honor), attending every show every night, "because, man, they do a different set every night, man, and plus… Eddie basically changes each song every time he does it, man!"

So, on this Friday night, as Pearl Jam prepared for their final show of the week, throngs of merch-covered men took over every bar and restaurant throughout downtown. Traffic was so unbearably slow, a few riders decided to get out and walk to their destination to save time. I was getting sick of the recycled small talk about traffic and concerts and Pearl Jam, so I was relieved when I found myself heading out of town into a residential neighborhood to pick up Clint.

My phone's navigation led me uphill along winding side streets, past brick ranches and detached garages. I arrived at a narrow two-story house. It was so narrow that it looked like it was supposed to be part of a row of townhouses, but the builders had given up after one unit. I stared at the tan brick house, wondering if our homes said anything about the type of people we were.

Clint's home looked fine from the street. It had no landscaping to speak of, not even trees or bushes in the yard. It was just a pile of bricks rising out of the mostly dead grass. There was a cement path connecting the front door to the sidewalk that was slowly being diminished by the overgrown grass on either side. Paint was chipped off the jet-black shudders bookending the windows, giving the home a rustic look, like a pair of faded jeans. If it were in an upscale neighborhood, the house would be a disastrous eyesore, yet it was the nicest looking property on its street.

Clint pulled the front door open and set a suitcase on the stoop, before disappearing momentarily back inside the house. I instinctively unbuckled and headed for the trunk, smiling at the thought of making an airport trip and avoiding downtown. When Clint re-emerged, he had two more full-size suitcases with him. This was no quick weekend trip.

Clint was tall with narrow shoulders and looked athletic. Long, well-toned arms extended out of his light gray Nike golf shirt and led two of his three suitcases down the three concrete steps in front of the house. He had jet-black hair wind-swept to the side, with just enough strands sticking up to make it seem like he looked this good on accident. His navy and gray Nike tennis shoes, paired with the jeans that looked pressed, made me wonder if he was the sort of person that always made sure his accessories matched his outfit before leaving the house. It was as if the mannequin from the sporting goods store's golf section was standing in front of me.

He took turns rolling each suitcase a little closer to me, like a one-man fireman's brigade. And each time he'd turn around for the other suitcase his head would swivel back and forth between the house, his suitcase, me, the ground, and back to the suitcases. He seemed anxious, like he was afraid something was off or that he'd forgotten an important item. When the front wheels of his largest suitcase caught on a crack in the sidewalk and fell forward, he jumped back like it was a grenade. False alarm. He set it upright and continued working his way toward me.

"Hi there," I tried, "are we heading to the airport?"

At first, he didn't respond, keeping his eyes on the two suitcases in front of him. As if the task required his full attention.

"Uh, yeah, the airport," he eventually stammered, trying to wrangle the first suitcase over the curb to my waiting hands, "and hi, sorry."

As he handed me the final suitcase, our eyes met just long enough for me to see that he wasn't worried about forgetting something. He was trying to hold back tears.

"Thanks," he managed, quickly turning away and sliding in the car. I finished tucking his bags inside the trunk, hopped back in the driver's seat, and set off for the airport.

I wanted to ask about the almost-tears, but I didn't know how to broach the subject. Clint was staring out the window, lost in his thoughts. I needed something, anything, to break the ice.

"Pearl Jam is playing tonight!" My not-so-smooth icebreaker shot out of my mouth like a cannonball without warning.

"Oh yeah?" He didn't move a muscle. He was unfazed by the artillery fire, off in his own world.

"Yeah, the traffic has been horrible with all their fans. Earlier, a few of my riders just decided…" I let the rest of my sentence trail off. Clint had no interest in conversation, so I gave up and returned my focus to navigating the thickening traffic.

Maybe it was the lack of a conversation partner, or perhaps that every radio station seemed to be playing Pearl Jam, but I tuned the radio to NPR, keeping it quiet enough to avoid disturbing my meditative passenger.

News headlines from throughout the week were being read with a certain journalistic monotone that I instantly recognized as Bill's. Striking a positive-not-perky tone in the tenor range, Bill's voice had a way of softly cradling harsher syllables, like catching a raw egg. His typical sentence structure involved methodically plodding through the first two-thirds with careful enunciation, a slight pause, and then cruising through the final third with the rising intonation of a kind question. The resulting gracefulness made you feel that you could trust him. That he was objective. A good journalist.

Listening to Bill host his weekly panel discussions on recent events, I came to feel like I knew him. I formed an image in my head of what he looked like. I imagined his facial expressions and body language as his interactions with his guests reverberated over the airwaves and found my car's speakers. Of course, the veil was lifted by looking up his picture online. People are never exactly like you imagine.

Bill asked his guests what they thought about Melania Trump's parents becoming citizens and what they might predict about Paul Manafort's trial outcome. But it was the panel's main topic of conversation - Trump's plan to create a new military branch called Space Force - that set Clint free from the gravitational force of his window and produced a chuckle.

"It's just so ridiculous," he said between snorts and chortles, "like we need to send armed assassins into space! I mean, who are they going to fight? Aliens?"

"Yeah seriously," I shot back, making sure to match his level of laughter.

"Wait, does this mean that you're *not* headed to Space Force Boot Camp?? I thought I was taking you to the airport because you had just enlisted!" My sarcasm connected. He laughed hard and saluted me through the mirror.

After his laughter died down, Clint leaned forward and grabbed the armrest of the passenger seat with his right hand. I still had to use the rear-view mirror to make eye contact but coming this close made it feel like we were friends catching up, not strangers sharing a taxi.

"Oh God, I needed that," he said. "It's been a bit of a rough week."

"A rough week," I repeated as a question, "why's that?"

"Well, the long and the short of it is, I got a job offer in San Diego, and my girlfriend and I have been fighting all week about whether I should take the job or stay here."

I connected the dots. "Ah, I see. So you're headed to California I take it."

"Yep."

"And your girlfriend isn't happy about that," I said definitively.

"No, that's the thing," he half-blurted out, "She was the one telling me to take the job."

"Oh ok," I said, as if I was all caught up now, "*you* didn't want to take this job…?"

"No, I wanted the job, but I didn't want to split up. She's staying here, and I just know that we won't last with the whole long-distance relationship thing. It's complicated, you know!?"

"Ahhhh, I see." I paused, trying to sound like a wise philosopher about to solve this poor man's life-long problem. "Ok, but explain one thing: why doesn't she just move to San Diego with you?"

I smiled triumphantly as he collapsed back into his seat and sighed.

"Family." His one-word response sounded sympathetic, like she didn't have a choice.

"Her family won't let her move?"

"No, it's not that. She's… uh… She's pregnant."

The word 'pregnant' landed hard.

"Oh," I said, still lost as to what the problem was.

"Yeah, and her family is here. Everyone- mom, sisters, aunts, uncles, cousins. There's no way I could even ask her to raise a child anywhere else."

"Ok, let me get this straight," I said, "So, your girlfriend is pregnant and she's not leaving her family, but she's still trying to convince you to take a job in a different state?!?" I paused briefly to soften my tone, hoping I wasn't prying into unfriendly territory.

"Is the baby yours?"

His response was delayed. This conversation had taken him back and he was starting to get emotional again.

"No, yeah," he half-whispered, wiping a tear from the corner of his eye, "the baby is mine. Of course."

I wanted to say the right thing, but I didn't know what the right thing was. I wasn't sure if I should help him feel ok about the circumstances or convince him to change his mind. The whole situation was still very confusing. The only thing I knew was that he needed me to be soft in that moment, so I exhaled loudly, shook my head sympathetically, and then cautiously asked for the details.

Clint explained that he had applied for the job well before they knew they were pregnant, and he knew that it would take some convincing for Aimee to ever leave her home. So, for weeks he had been gushing about the job. He'd been talking up the pay and the benefits. He'd been sending her articles about living on a sailboat, texting her images of sunsets at the beach in southern California, and giving her talking points to use with her family. He knew he had to convince her, so he went overboard, exaggerating all the positives and downplaying all the negatives. He executed a near-flawless two-month marketing campaign that convinced everyone in his life that this job, in San Diego, was the chance to live his dreams. And so, when Aimee's period was late the day before his final interview, and when the pregnancy test had two scratchy lines six hours before he received his offer letter, Clint found himself in a difficult position.

His dreams shape-shifted instantly. His heart did a U-turn and he knew he needed to make his case for staying here. But, as Clint put together his briefs and prepared his opening statement, he looked over at the prosecuting attorney and realized he wasn't arguing with Aimee, he was arguing against himself. Every statement he'd made. Every manipulative question he'd used to paint a picture of paradise. Every link he pasted into text messages. It all made for compelling evidence. He knew Aimee was a tough judge and that this was an open-shut case.

The trial lasted five days, each day consisting of a short, fiery exchange in the morning and a long-drawn-out debate after work. Clint had an impossible challenge. With all the facts of the case against him, he had to convince Aimee that his future would be free of resentment. That he'd never grow bitter wishing for the life he could've had in San Diego. That he wouldn't turn into Aimee's father.

July 15th, 1988

Marshall had always dreamed of becoming a civil rights lawyer. While other kids turned in book reports on Martin Luther King Jr. or Rosa Parks, he studied up on Charles Hamilton Houston, Jack Greenberg, and his namesake - Thurgood Marshall. He'd spent his family's modest life savings to get through college, had used every waking moment studying to get good grades, and had now been accepted at Howard University School of Law. He was a first-generation college student, a black man about to attend a famous HBCU for law school, and a dreamer with visions of sitting on the US Supreme Court someday. But, for now, he had a different decision to make.

His girlfriend was pregnant.

Debbie and Marshall had been hot and cold for the entire six months they'd been together, mostly due to their own decision avoidance. They knew Marshall was moving across the country at the end of the summer, but Debbie had been oscillating between breaking up with him and considering the possibility of following him to D.C.

Sitting across from Debbie's parents at their kitchen table, less than twenty-four hours after the doctor visit, Marshall had to decide if he was going to marry Debbie or, as her dad had put it, "selfishly abdicate his responsibility and abandon his child."

He felt trapped. Everyone just expected Marshall to give up everything in an instant. His hopes and dreams were being ripped away from him. To marry Debbie meant giving up on law school. Debbie certainly couldn't work, and there was no way he could support a family and go to school at the same time. But to leave Debbie meant marking her with a scarlet 'A' within her community and forcing her to rely on the goodwill of others to survive. He knew it was the right thing to do.

Two hours later they had planned a wedding.

Five days later he started work at his future father-in-law's car repair shop.

Three weeks later he and Debbie were married.

Nine months later Aimee was born.

Seven years later he walked out the door and never came back.

August 5th, 2018 - 10:00pm

Aimee's only memories of her father had come from watching him replace windshields and buff out scratches at her grandpa's repair shop. According to her mom, it had been a good enough job, for the most part. It paid enough to cover the bills, he was treated fairly by Grandpa, and her dad didn't even mind the work. It just wasn't law school.

Aimee had heard the story enough times from her mom to have it memorized. In fact, she had told Clint the story enough times that he probably had memorized it, too. And yet, he still wasn't getting it. They were going on day three, hour two of this fight, and she was exhausted.

"Have you thought about money," Clint offered, "how are you going to pay for grad school? Child support won't be enough."

"Look," she yelled at his back as Clint headed toward the fridge, "I can figure out the finances. I'm not changing my mind on this. If you stay here because of me, you'll resent me. And I don't want to be the straw that breaks your neck."

Clint emerged from the kitchen carrying a newly opened beer, a self-assured smirk appearing just under the shadow line from his golf hat.

"First of all," he began, like he was cross-examining the witness, "that's not how you use that phrase."

"What phrase?"

"The straw that broke the camel's back."

"The what? I never said that!"

"You're right. You never said that, because if you had said *that* you would've used the phrase correctly."

"Whatever."

"But even then, it wouldn't apply to this situation. There haven't been any previous straws."

Aimee raised her voice to cut through this useless caveat. "What the hell are you even talking about?!"

"I'm just trying to say that I won't resent you if I stay here."

"It doesn't work like that, Clint. It's not that easy. You can't just decide to not resent me."

"Well," Clint snapped back, almost shouting, "*you* can't just decide that I *will* resent you!"

They stared at each other, silent and expressionless for a moment. Aimee let out a slow sigh.

"Clint... I know that you think you'd be able to stay here, and everything would just continue on as normal. I know that you *think* you won't constantly dwell on the chance you had to work at a golf technology company and be a golf pro at a real country club in your dream location. I know that you *think* you can be happy supporting me through grad school, by working at the sporting goods store--"

"And being with you! And raising our baby," Clint interjected.

"Yes, yes, I know. All of those things. I know that you think you'll be happy and that you won't grow to resent me or our kid. But…"

"But what?!"

"But I also know what will really happen, eventually."

"What?"

"Eventually, you'll… you'll get tired of all this. You'll get sick of it. You'll decide it's time to do what *you* want for once. Clint - eventually… you'll leave."

He flinched, hurt by her absolute certainty about his future actions.

"That's not fair," he managed to say, keeping his eyes pointed at the floor, "you don't know that."

"Trust me," Aimee said, "I know. And I'm not going to let our child lose a parent. Better to never have a dad than to lose one before you even turn seven."

Clint realized in that moment just how hopeless his case was. There was literally nothing he could do to convince her that *this life* was what he truly wanted, and a panic started to settle in. It was just a marble-sized knot, at first, spinning in his stomach. But it started to spread, winning organs and muscles to its cause, taking over his torso, tranquilizing his legs. What was he supposed to do? Should he just give in?

Just accept this diagnosis of future bitterness? Was he going to give up on them? On being a father?

Focusing on each micro-movement, Clint managed to navigate his numb body over to the couch and sit down next to Aimee. He wiped the mixture of snot and tears off his upper lip with the back of his hand, and searched for some part of him, any part, that was resisting the panic. Just when he was ready to cave, he found an ounce of resolve, holding out hope in his fingertips. He dug the nails of his middle fingers into his thumbs, willing them to spread their strength. It was working. The lump in his throat shrunk and his legs started to feel stable. "This might be my only chance," he kept repeating in his head. He took a deep breath, and then stood up to deliver his closing argument.

"Aimee," he begged, "Please believe me when I say this: I love you! And I will love our baby too, with everything I have." He let the tears flow as he slowly brought his gaze up to her face. "And I don't know what will happen in the future, but I know one thing… I am not your dad."

He paused and then repeated for emphasis, "I am not your dad."

Those were the last words either spoke that night, but over the next twenty-four hours, Aimee tried and tried to believe Clint. She let herself picture them as a family of three, hosting birthday parties and going to school functions. She rehearsed their happiest moments together as a couple, surprised at the highlight reel that came to her. The documentary marathon from two summers ago that inspired Aimee to go back and finish her degree. The round of putt-

putt where she won by three strokes and accidentally hit him in the shin with her backswing. The trip to Phoenix where Clint placed second in the amateur golf tournament, and they spent all of his winnings to book the best hotel suite in town for two nights. But it was the final memory - walking the beach in San Diego the night before his final interview - that shattered her fragile momentum.

The whole evening had felt like a dream. They had flown down in the afternoon so Clint could take her to his favorite restaurant. He'd made this trip dozens of times. Golfed at Torrey Pines and every other course within a two-hour drive. Tested each beach at sunset. Every restaurant's dinner menu. This night had to be perfect.

He made his sales pitch over dinner. He had salmon, Aimee ordered lobster. Clint explained what he'd be doing for this company. He reminisced about past golf tournaments and the great experiences they'd had together because of them. He reminded her how rare it was for a black man to get opportunities like this. Especially in the world of golf. Then he took her for a walk on the beach.

Feeling the sand in-between their toes and listening to the waves crashing ashore, they walked hand-in-hand, visualizing their future in this paradise. He walked her a half-mile south of the restaurant, to a pier sticking out over the Pacific.

"So, what do you say?" He asked, as they reached the end of the pier.

"What do I say to what?"

"To this question." Clint went down to a knee.

"Wait, what are you doing?"

"I'm asking you something."

"But I thought we were waiting on that."

He smiled up at her. "Just listen, Aimee. I love you. Really love you. And I don't have a ring yet, so I'm not going to ask you that. Yet."

He paused for effect.

"And until that comes, I have another question. Will you move to San Diego with me?"

"If you get this job, you mean?"

"*When* I get this job, it's going to be a life-changing thing. And I want it to change *our* lives. Together. I want you to come with me. To join me in this life. Here in the best place on earth."

Aimee responded as if it were a marriage proposal, lifting him off his knee and kissing him deeply.

The memory brought a smile to her face. They'd never been happier. But how was she to determine which part of their happiness was tied to their relationship, and which part was just sitting on the shoulders of his dreams? Dreams of living in a warm, sunny, golf-obsessed location, working the perfect job, and competing in tournaments? How was she to calculate how much of that loss would be made up for by a child? How was she to imagine a future with him that didn't resemble the only story of dreams, pregnancies, and family she'd ever known?!?

Friday, August 10th, 2018 - 8:38pm

The car came to a stop, a half-mile before the airport's exit, as they became swallowed by the worst traffic jam Clint could remember. All six lanes were at a complete standstill, and there was no movement up ahead as far as he could see. The driver muttered under his breath and fiddled with the radio. Clint went back to staring out his window at nothing in particular.

In his mind, he kept replaying the conversations with Aimee throughout the past week, wondering what he could've said differently. If he could've convinced her. Her last words on the matter echoed in his head:

"I want to believe you, Clint, but every time I close my eyes and imagine the future I see the same thing - you leaving for California."

He was stuck. In traffic. In Aimee's version of their future. In a future without the person he loved and without the chance to get to know their child.

After a few minutes of immobility, Clint's thoughts were brought back to the scene unfolding on the highway, all around the car. He looked at everything through the windshield, like it was a television. In fact, it was starting to look like a movie scene. An action thriller about an alien invasion, maybe.

A handful of cars had tried to skirt around traffic by driving on the shoulder, but they were just as stuck as everyone else. Some vehicles had their hazards on. Most had shifted into park. Four car-lengths ahead, a silver Chevy

Cavalier had somehow managed to be turned sideways, parked across most of two lanes.

Clint rolled down his window instinctively, as if he could discover the source of the backup through listening. He took in the scene. The angst of delayed plans. The claustrophobia of being trapped by hundreds of bumpers. The nervous energy causing some to get out of their cars and stretch or crane their necks, trying to see miles ahead.

In a traffic jam, it's important to remain convinced, no matter how delusional, that something can be done. If only you get out for a better look, or double check the pressure in your tires, things will be moving soon. Clint had no such hope. Instead, he wished for traffic to get worse. He needed to miss this flight. He needed one more chance to convince Aimee. He knew exactly what he'd say this time.

Aimee couldn't stop pacing in her living room. Her bare feet were leaving a trail in the carpet. An arc from the east wall to the west, her hopes rising and falling like the sun that follows the same path. On the east wall of the room there was a framed picture of her and Clint. A candid shot of them laughing in her mom's backyard. As she neared this side of the room Aimee knew she was being paranoid and judgmental and absurd. She wanted to be with Clint, and she needed to stop torpedoing the relationship. On the other coast, where Clint's six amateur golf trophies filled the middle shelf of a bookcase, she saw what made Clint happy and she knew firsthand just how painful it was to have a dream rupture a family. Both sides had validity and she believed both coasts equally. She was convinced Clint would resent her and the baby, making life miserable before and after his inevitable departure. But she was just as convinced that they belonged together. That they could be happy and figure it out.

Maybe that's just how life worked. Maybe the whole world was filled with resentful people who had dared to try on the one hand, and lonely people who'd known better on the other. You can only have happiness if you're willing for it to be ripped out of your hands later. Joy comes in partial, fleeting pieces. Aimee's east or west was a choice between a short-lived joyride or protecting herself from its inevitable crash landing, and she was a mother now. She had to protect her baby.

Clint slid his vibrating phone out of his pocket, hoping it was Aimee inviting him back. Instead, it was a notification from American Airlines. His flight had been canceled. What was going on? They hadn't moved an inch in over fifteen minutes, and they were still at least a mile from the airport. He knew what bad traffic felt like, but this was something else entirely.

"Any clue what's going on?" He casually tossed the question to the driver, trying not to sound as panicked and hemmed in as he felt inside.

"No idea," the driver said, "maybe a major accident or something. I've never seen it this bad before."

"My flight just got canceled," Clint offered, almost to himself. A clue that might help solve the mystery in front of them.

The driver turned up the radio so they could listen along to the news, and they both grabbed their phones. Facebook and Instagram were full of typical Friday night posts - group selfies at a bar in capitol hill, bathroom mirror shots showing off tonight's chosen outfits, or close-up pictures of Pearl Jam tickets, bragging about having on-field seats. Nothing about four-thousand parked cars on the highway outside the airport.

Scrolling through Twitter, Clint got sidetracked by his friend's re-tweet of a live news update about a hijacking. The way he saw it, any headline with "hijacking" in the title gets an automatic read. It took Clint all of four seconds on the twitter stream to see the connection. His breath caught in the back of his throat. About ninety minutes earlier, someone had hijacked a plane at SeaTac - one mile away from where he was stuck in traffic. The whole airport was on lock-down.

Aimee couldn't get Clint's final appeal out of her mind.

"Aimee - I am not your dad."

That was never really in question. Aimee had little firsthand experience of her father, but it was enough to form a Grand Canyon-sized gap between Clint and him.

"I *know* you're not my dad," Aimee said out loud to the empty room, "but my dad's not the only one." She instinctively started through the mental list of names to prove her point - her aunt's ex-husband, her old youth leader, her favorite teacher from middle school - when it struck her that none of the examples she had were from her own generation. She stopped pacing and let the realization materialize. The most basic rule of life, which had been ingrained in her from her earliest days, was just that - *ingrained*. It was one of the orthodoxies she had been indoctrinated with, so deeply and so powerfully that she had mistaken it for universal truth. Men leave. That's just how the world works. But she hadn't learned that from *her* experience. It had been taught to her.

The problem, she realized, wasn't that Clint might turn out like her dad. It was that Aimee had already become her mom.

Her instincts, her fears, her worldview - they were all stemming from her mom's experience, as if it were her own. Her mom had done her job well. She had pulled Aimee in tight and protected them from the harsh and difficult world they lived in. Don't trust. Don't rely on anyone, because then you'll end up alone and heartbroken. But now, it was time for Aimee to set herself free. To protect her own child now. From a life lived in fear of someone else's pain.

Aimee felt her shoulders unwind from the clenched hunch she didn't know they were in. She took a deep breath in and slowly rolled her head back until she was looking at the popcorn ceiling. This was the first full breath she'd taken in weeks, and it took over every inch of her body. Aimee was free.

Her finger hovered over Clint's name on her phone. Aimee was ready to talk this through and give it a try, but she also wondered if he would even want to talk to her right now. Would he even take her call? She knew things did not go well this week, and he was probably already boarding his plane, or in the air. Not great timing.

She inhaled sharply and tapped the screen, but a notification came sliding down from the top of the screen, in between her finger and Clint's name. She had a text message. It was from her mom.

"TURN ON THE NEWS! SOMEONE HIJACKED A PLANE AT SEATAC!"

Aimee's left hand shot to her mouth, trying to stop the impending vomit, while her right clutched her stomach. It felt like someone had twisted her intestines inside-out. Her phone fell to the floor, its bottom right corner bouncing off the laminate. A thin crack in the screen crept from the impact point to the opposite corner, leaving a lightning bolt-shaped reminder of this moment, but Aimee didn't notice.

Out of all the airports in the world, and all the flights coming and going, there was a 0.001% chance the hijacker was on Clint's flight - but Aimee was sure that's what had happened. This was the evil way the universe worked when someone made a mistake like she had this week. It was Karma. She had been too short-sighted, too scared to open her mind and her life to Clint and now he was gone forever. Aimee collapsed to the floor sobbing, her cheek pressed against the cool vinyl as her tears and mucus pooled under her nose. She curled her legs up toward her chest and stared at her dark phone, laying inches from her. How she wished she could go back in time. She would call him hours earlier, tell him she'd changed her mind, and beg him not to get on his flight.

Clint was stammering incoherently in the back seat, saying half-sentences about the news and planes, when the radio gave a low monotone beep and interrupted the replay of Bill's weekly news round-up.

"We apologize for interrupting our normal programming," she began, "but we want to share some tragic news with you, our listeners." She sounded nervous, like her training as a news anchor was fighting with her panic. Maybe she'd never had to give the news with so little prep time before, or perhaps she was worried about people she loved that were affected.

"Please be advised that this story is still developing, and we will try to give you further information the moment we receive it. Also, what I am about to share may be triggering to some and may not be suitable for listeners of all ages. With that said, my name is Paige Bronson, and this is a news bulletin."

She paused. To collect herself? For dramatic effect?

"At approximately 7:30pm, an aircraft was hijacked at SeaTac International Airport. The plane did not have any passengers. Apparently, it was sitting empty in a hangar, when a maintenance worker entered the cockpit, taxied the plane, and took off. The maintenance worker's identity is being kept private for the time being. Here's what we know so far: The aircraft was a Horizon Air Bombardier Q400 - that's a propeller plane which I'm told is mostly used for short-distance passenger routes between Seattle and surrounding cities. It was not undergoing maintenance or being used but was parked in a hangar on the north end of the airport. Though Air Traffic Control could not establish radio contact prior to the unauthorized takeoff, they were able to keep in radio communication throughout most of the flight. Shortly after the stolen plane was airborne, the Air National Guard responded. The following will be read directly from their statement regarding their actions.

Given the security threat to the highly populated area around SeaTac, the crowds gathering for a concert at SafeCo Field, and the possibility of intent to harm, we scrambled two fighter jets as soon as we were informed of the incident at SeaTac. We were in communication with the person piloting the plane, through Air Traffic Control, attempting to ascertain his intentions and/or flight path. We were prepared to shoot down the aircraft if and when it presented itself as a threat.

That was a statement from the Air National Guard regarding the hijacking of an empty passenger plane from SeaTac this evening. Fortunately, the fighter jets did not have to shoot the plane down as the mechanic who stole the plane did not do so as an act of terrorism. However, this story does end in tragedy. As made clear throughout the pilot's radio conversation with the tower, the mechanic involved was suffering from depression and stole the plane in order to commit suicide. He described himself as a 'broken man' and repeatedly rebuffed the encouragement from the authorities to land the plane safely at Joint Base Lewis-McChord. Instead, he attempted to perform barrel-rolls, somersaults, and other aerial maneuvers with the aircraft, until just moments ago, when he ended his life by crashing the stolen plane into the Puget Sound.

We will continue to update you on this developing story throughout the evening."

Clint and I sat in shocked silence for a full minute. The highway all around us was completely full and eerily silent. The reality of the situation was slowly setting in. This was not a movie set. Someone actually stole a plane, not far from where we were parked, and used it to end his own life. And the thousands of us - *millions?* - affected by this were sitting still, parked next to a sign that said, "Speed Limit 60MPH", staring at the chaos around us, trying to wake up from the dream. What had just happened? What were we supposed to do now? Just drive off and go home? Try again tomorrow? How could a plane even get stolen, anyway?

Then, just as the dust began to settle and I was almost coming out of the fog, Clint lurched his phone forward into my line of sight. He had found the audio recording of the air traffic controller's radio conversation with the hijacker. We looked at each other for a second, feeling like our hands were on the latch of Pandora's box. Then, with the slightest nod of my head, I signaled that I was ready. He turned up the phone's volume to the max and pushed play.

The phone's vibrations tickled her cheekbones. Through her tears she could barely read the blurry letters traversing the new cracks in the screen. Clint was calling. It took Aimee three thumb swipes over the newly cracked screen to answer. She tapped to put the call on speaker, closed her eyes, and then laid her head back down on the tile floor. Clint's voice had a tone she hadn't heard before and he wasn't making any sense, talking about a maintenance worker and not wanting to do somersaults alone, but she didn't care. Hearing his voice meant he was alive and that made her smile wide enough to taste the salt in her tears pooling around her.

She wanted to explain everything, but she couldn't focus. Everything was a swirling gray and her whole head was vibrating from the mixture of fear, regret, joy, and emotional exhaustion. Judging by the frantic rant Clint was on, Aimee assumed he felt the same way. She curled herself into a ball, brought her phone right up against her cheek, and interrupted Clint.

"Clint! Clint, just listen... listen for a sec..."

Clint stopped mid-sentence and the line went quiet.

"Clint, listen. I'm sorry. I'm sorry." Aimee wondered if Clint could hear the quiver in her voice.

"Clint... You're not my dad. You're my mom. No, wait... I didn't mean that. I meant you're not my dad, *I'm* my mom."

"What? What does that mean?" Clint asked.

Aimee chuckled to herself. They were both hysterical and not making any sense.

"It means I love you and I want you to stay."

Aimee sensed Clint's relief. New evidence had presented itself. The jury did not need to deliberate.

So, as she hit a final wall of exhaustion, Aimee closed her eyes and sleepily whispered the final sentence:

"Clint... come home."

BREATH

5:22 PM

I didn't recognize what I had seen until a few seconds after it had passed. Motorcycles look different from the underside, and I was used to seeing them with their wheels on the ground. This fiery orange Harley-Davidson Road Glide two-seater was flying through the air, end over end like a kicked football, about to land in the ditch running along the side of the road. I heard a loud scraping sound as its handlebars and front wheel collided with the cement shoulder, and then it bounced slightly, flipping over one last time into the ditch. No explosion like the movies.

Then the second realization hit me - there was no rider. I had already slowed down to a crawl, my subconscious taking over the driving duties while I gawked, so I eased forward ever so slowly, my eyes scanning back and forth. As I reached the crest of the hill, the distinct smell of a vehicle accident invaded my car and overloaded my senses. A mixture of burnt rubber and various motor fluids. My gaze followed the black skid marks in front of me and there, lying still at the far end of the tire tracks, was a body.

1:38 PM

Grandpa was dying. That was the gist of the phone call from Mom. Not her father, though. Dad's dad. And so, even though my father and I were in a six-month-long fight, not having spoken to each other in 113 days, and even though he didn't find it important enough to share this news with me himself - according to my mother, I needed to put all that aside and call him. He was going to lose his father soon, and she was sure he'd appreciate the gesture.

Our fight had started small - arguing about whether a football team should change its name. He was a long-time fan and felt plenty of nostalgia. I couldn't care less about the traditions of the past and considered the current name racist. But before long, our tiff expanded to other topics. Immigration policies, recreational marijuana, dress codes in restaurants, fossil fuels, pronoun usage, and the "attempts by universities and academics to indoctrinate young minds with anti-American lies." It became the representative for any and all disagreements between us, allowing us to vent our anger at the generational differences or the other's political persuasion.

My Mom, always the peacekeeper, was distraught. Partly because she sided with her husband on most things and that meant her son was "in the wrong," but more so because it felt like her family was being torn apart. The thought occurred to me, even if only for a second, that she could be making up this story about Grandpa. That she might be manipulating me. Pulling the strings from the shadows. Trying to force a cease fire.

I told her I would call him and then immediately started brainstorming excuses to use for why I hadn't. I thought about how he should be the one to call and apologize, and about how I hoped Grandpa's death would show him how hard life can be when a son has his relationship with his father abruptly cut off. I knew I was being selfish and immature. But so was he.

2:19 PM

I needed to do something to clear my head. Something before my thoughts swirled into anger and my victimization got out of control. So, I grabbed my keys and went for a drive. I hoped my passengers would be a welcome distraction from the ludicrous fantasy argument I was having with my mind's projection of my dad. But, for the first two and a half hours, the conversations all seemed to gravitate toward families.

Mark, an electrician from Virginia, told me all about his month-long visit to his mother and how he was helping her deal with the death of her husband - Mark's stepfather. Then Monique shared the highlights from the Alaskan cruise she'd just disembarked from, with fourteen other members of her family. Sharon had lost both of her parents to cancer over the past year. Liz had never met her dad. Ty was helping his father get settled in a nursing home. I couldn't get away from parent-child relationships. It was as if my situation was somehow following me and forcing itself into every encounter.

4:58 PM

I dropped Ty off and decided to turn off the app for a little while and just drive alone. I was already on the outskirts of the suburbs, so I took the opportunity to explore new roads and areas I'd never seen before. I chose an unfamiliar route heading east, flanked by grassy fields and tall thick pine trees.

There's always been something peaceful about driving. Windows down. Late afternoon sun. Favorite music turned up loud. After singing along to four or five songs, I turned off the music and leaned my head slightly out the window. With no traffic, I was free to take in the beauty surrounding me. Rolling foothills, dotted with trees, spread out in front of me, the Cascades towering over them up ahead. The road curved around to the right and then began climbing a hill. The higher I climbed, the more I could see of the flatland to my right, but the hill was steep enough that I had no visibility of any vehicles coming at me, climbing the other side. An orange flash caught my eye, jerking me awake from the almost dream-like state I had slipped into.

I didn't recognize what I had seen until a few seconds after it had passed. Motorcycles look different from the underside, and I was used to seeing them with their wheels on the ground. This fiery orange Harley-Davidson Road Glide two-seater was flying through the air, end over end, like a kicked football, about to land in the ditch running along the side of the road. I heard a loud scraping sound as its handlebars and front wheel collided with the cement shoulder, and then it bounced slightly, flipping over one last time into the ditch. No explosion like the movies.

Then the second realization hit me - there was no rider. I had already slowed down to a crawl, my subconscious taking over the driving duties while I gawked, so I eased forward ever so slowly, my eyes scanning back and forth. As I reached the crest of the hill, the distinct smell of a vehicle accident invaded my car and overloaded my senses. A mixture of burnt rubber and various motor fluids. My gaze followed the black skid marks in front of me and there, lying still at the far end of the tire tracks, was a body.

I'd never seen an accident before. Well, I'd seen the aftermath of accidents and a few "fender-benders" - including the two I'd been in. But I'd never seen a true high-speed accident in real time. I froze, and my brain went through a series of thoughts, all within a micro-second.

I am woefully unprepared for this. Why don't I know what to do? How come in movies and on TV they always know what to do in situations like this? Is that person dead? What if they're dead? What do I do then? What do I do if they're alive?

The bike-less rider was laying right in the middle of the road, half of their body in each lane. I was worried about them getting run over. I had slowed down because of the flying motorcycle, but someone else coming up that hill might not see the body if they're coming over the hill at full speed. Or they might see the body, but not have enough time to react. I put my car in reverse, backing it up to the crest of the hill, confident it was visible for a full half-mile behind me, and then I turned on my hazards and put it in park.

"Well," I said out loud to myself, trying to pump myself up, "I guess this is my moment to shine."

I opened the car door and began the walk down the hill to where the body was. I felt nervous. Hands trembling. Mouth dry. Heart racing. I was either still in shock from my up-close view of the motorcycle's destruction, or terrified of what I would find at the bottom of the hill. Or both. Memories I had long forgotten resurfaced. The three worst accident scenes I'd ever witnessed.

Iowa

In Iowa, you can see a long way. Which is why, after a two-hour wait, when we finally got to the top of the small hill, I could see all ninety cars involved in the pileup. The winter storm had been a rough one, and with blustering winds blinding drivers, two semi-trucks jack-knifing across the entire roadway started a chain reaction that lasted as long as the storm. Ninety cars twisted sideways, flipped upside-down, dented, door-less, and splintered. Just enough of the left shoulder plowed clean to allow the next morning's travelers to pass by single file.

Atlanta

Two details stick out in my memory. The fingers and the sun. The traffic jam ensured I was passing the scene at only five miles per hour. The two black SUV's were less than fifteen feet away. The trunk of one and the engine block of the other smashed. Flattened to nothing. All four visible windows had burn marks surrounding them. The vehicles had been on fire. And hanging out the back window - arms. Arms and shoulders and a head with perfect pigtails. And wide-spread fingers frozen in place. The arms weren't hanging. They were reaching. And between all of it, flares of the sun's golden late afternoon light, muting all colors and coating the whole scene in a surreal glow. Like an artistic passing drone shot.

Indiana

Sometimes you see something that, in and of itself, is so remarkable and astounding you are incapable of describing it to others. But I'll try. An early 2000's Honda Accord was cut in half, from bumper to bumper. There was no evidence suggesting *what* exactly cut it in half, but it looked as if someone had taken the world's largest and sharpest buzz saw, and carefully separated the driver's side from the passenger's. The sight haunts my curiosity to this day.

At sixty feet away, I could see that the rider's helmet had somehow flown off his head. It was laying further down the hill by the side of the road. At fifty feet, it was clear by the awkward position it was in, that his right leg was broken. At thirty feet I saw blood on the rider's otherwise thick dark brown beard. At twenty feet, scrapes on his exposed torso, where his jacket and shirt had been shredded. At ten feet tears in his eyes. At five the rhythmic rising and falling in his chest from breathing. He was alive.

Standing next to the rider, I was searching for the right thing to say. He shifted his eyes to look at me, without moving a single neck muscle.

"I saw your bike," I started, with far too much enthusiasm and positivity for the situation, "it landed up over the hill."

The rider didn't respond. I said a quick prayer in my head and tried again.

"Are you OK?" As soon as I said the words, I felt the ridiculousness of them. Of course he's not OK.

With some effort, he whispered a breathy reply through gritted teeth.

"Can you call an ambulance?"

I was so embarrassed I didn't say a word. I just started feeling my pockets to find my phone. How stupid was I, that I didn't even think to call 911?! No matter how unprepared I was for a situation like this, everybody knows to call an ambulance! What was I thinking!? What was my plan? To pull some sort of "Good Samaritan" move? To save his life somehow with my zero training or expertise?

My self-flagellation was interrupted by a more pressing concern - my phone was not in my pockets. Realizing I must've left it in the car, I turned around and took off running up the hill, murmuring insults to myself.

"No! No! No! You idiot!"

"Get it together, man!"

Just as I was running out of breath, about two-thirds of the way back to the car, it occurred to me that I hadn't even responded to the rider. He'd asked me to call an ambulance, to which I said nothing, randomly patted down all the pockets of my clothing, and then promptly turned around and ran away. I didn't want him to think I was abandoning him, leaving him to die alone, and I didn't want him to try and move his body to make the call himself and make his injuries worse. So, I stopped, took a few seconds with my hands on my knees to catch my breath, then whipped around and yelled down to him.

"Stay right there! I'm going to grab my phone so I can call 911!" More mumbling as I jogged the rest of the way to the car.

"You're making this worse. 'Stay right there!?' Really? Do you hear yourself? Where is he going to go?!"

I had to put my phone on speaker as I tried to explain to the emergency dispatch where we were. I had no idea, but I had just enough cell service to pull up the map and describe it to them. I headed back to the rider and let him know that they were on their way.

"Thank you," he breathed at me. An awkward silence followed as he was focused on breathing, and I was trying not to screw this up further. I looked over the scene in front of me and realized just how big this motorcyclist was.

I hadn't noticed it before, probably because even a tall person doesn't take up very much space compared to a two-lane road; but, when I tried to envision how long my body would be laying down next to him, I figured he was probably at least six feet four. The same height and basic build as my dad. He had broad shoulders, both probably injured based on the fact that he wasn't moving his arms at all, and a thick neck, partially hidden by the beard. His two tree-trunk thighs filled out black motorcycle pants and his one not-broken leg seamlessly led to tan high-top boots.

I was trying to imagine what his NFL career must have been like, or if he was some mobster's bodyguard, when I realized the body was talking to me. His half-whisper pulled me out of my daydream, but I was too late to catch what he was saying.

"Oh, I'm sorry," I said, "what was that?"

"My name… is Gary."

Over the next eight minutes, Gary told me all about his life as a soon-to-be divorced father of two. My focus oscillated between the slow stream of blood escaping his left ear and his story, trying to catch all the details. He and Kelly were splitting up after seventeen years. They were already separated. He hadn't seen her in months. There was no specific reason for their marriage ending, like an affair or an unforgivable reaction during a fight. It was just the years of drifting apart. They had no connection left. No reason to stay together, now that the kids were teenagers. Interestingly enough, he shared, in the half-second leading up to the crash, it wasn't Dillon or Sam that flashed before his eyes. It was Kelly. Gary was shocked by that. In the moment of his impending death, his brain flooded him with an emotional energy spike that would jolt him into focused action and maybe save his life, and the person his subconscious decided would create the strongest will to live - the person he'd most want to stay alive for - was the woman his conscious-self stopped caring about months ago.

Gary wasn't normally a mystical person. He didn't believe in horoscopes or "offering things out to the universe." But then again, Gary wasn't normally getting nudges from his subconscious due to near-death experiences. Who was he to question this inner voice?! This deep instinct?! And beyond that, he explained, over the last several minutes laying here on the ground - ribs probably fractured, leg definitely broken - he was getting clarity. With every passing second, his heart grew stronger in its affirmation of this new instinctive feeling. This realization that he still loved his wife. I resisted the urge to share my concerns about one's judgment when they are plastered on the road in shock. Gary cried harder as he lamented the way he and Kelly had grown distant. Then he asked for my help.

"Can you," he started before a brief shivering breathy sob cut him off. "Can you call her for me?"

What?! He wants me to call his estranged, soon-to-be-ex-wife?!

"My phone… my phone is probably…" Another shiver. "My phone is probably destroyed. It was on the bike. So, can you call her? I need her to know I'm sorry."

What exactly am I supposed to say if I call her? "Hi, Kelly, is it? Yeah, I'm a total stranger to both of you, but I think you and Gary should give it another go. I mean, your husband, who was bored with you and couldn't care less about you an hour ago, crashed his motorcycle, probably hit his head, and all of a sudden, he's a changed man. He wants to make things work. What do you think?"

Absolutely not! I am not getting involved in this.

"Call her? Like, me call Kelly for you," I asked.

"Yeah, on your phone."

"Uh, sure. No, yeah, I can call her," I said, pulling my cell phone back out. "What's her number?"

As Gary tried to remember the phone number and recite it to me, his whispers were drowned out by the sirens of the approaching ambulance.

I was saved.

Once the ambulance had navigated around my parked car at the top of the hill, they mercifully shut off the siren. My ear drums were vibrating, but I became aware of a different sensation. My left hand was warm and a little numb. I looked down and I saw Gary's man-paw enveloping my entire hand and wrist. Only my thumb was visible. I wondered how long we'd been holding hands, as the EMT's gently pushed me aside to begin assisting Gary.

From a few steps back, I watched as they talked with him, adjusted his leg some while he cried out in pain, and eventually loaded him onto a stretcher and took him away. He kept his left arm slightly outstretched throughout the entire process, his hand reaching just a little in my direction. A phantom gesture. A subconscious tick. But it left an imprint on my memory of those moments.

I kept replaying the events over and over in my head as I walked up to my car and began to drive nowhere in particular. Something just out of focus was nagging at me. Knocking on my mind, trying to be heard. But I couldn't materialize it. I followed the road around a few more bends, noticing that the sun was almost setting, before succumbing to the growling in my stomach and pulling into the parking lot of a roadside bar.

Everyone was talking to their tablemates. Dozens of gossipers or storytellers or pseudo-journalists. Sitting in the back-right corner booth, the collective din blanketed me in anonymity. I sank further into my dark green cushioned seat, stretching the torn plastic-like fabric. It wasn't a large room, but it didn't feel cramped. The U-shaped bar intruded the space from the wall to my right, with booths up against the three other walls and tables in between. The few fluorescent light bulbs that weren't burned out or missing gave a spotty, subtly flickering glow to the room, which was reinforced by the neon beer logo lights scattered around. All in all, it was exactly what you'd expect in a dive bar, and it was full of life.

I ordered a burger and fries and tried to put Gary out of my mind. As I eavesdropped on a few conversations around me, one voice was cutting through the noise and kept grabbing my attention. Sitting at the counter facing me, right on the corner before it turned and ran parallel to the kitchen, a woman was arguing with her father. She looked to be in her fifties, tall with short brown hair. She was wearing a red sweater over a white blouse and ruby-colored dangling earrings matching her sweater. In fact, her cheeks practically matched her sweater, too. She was very upset with her dad, and, thanks to her shrill piercing voice, I could hear every word.

"You always do this," she was saying, "You know, Dad? Here I'm, trying to do something nice. I thought tonight could just be friendly! No fighting, no arguing. But no, you can't let us have one night of peace, can you!?"

I could tell, mostly from experience, that she was trying to get a rise out of her dad, but he wasn't responding at all. She just kept going. Undaunted by his silence. He sat perfectly still, leaning forward slightly and staring straight ahead. An unmoving buoy in the bar's ocean of chaos. An unmoving buoy whose face was turning purple. And who's eyes were bulging. He was choking.

The daughter's scream for help silenced the whole room.

"Someone Help! Dad!? Dad...?! Chip!? Dad, can you hear me?!?"

Chip's eyes were rolling back in his head, and he was slipping into unconsciousness. She yelled for a doctor. I desperately wanted to look away. Or run away. But I couldn't move. My entire body was cement.

A mid-thirties woman squeezed through the small crowd that had encircled Chip's stool, identifying herself as a nurse. She started giving out instructions. Two muscular men were supposed to raise Chip out of his seat and hold him upright, while the nurse performed the Heimlich. As they pulled Chip's mostly limp body upright, my chest tightened, and my breath caught. Sitting down, this man looked like a total stranger. But standing up, Chip looked like the long-lost twin of my grandfather. The man who was lying in a hospital bed, inching closer to the end of his life.

Chip had become fully unconscious, but the two men held firm. The nurse slid behind Chip and reached her arms around his torso. She was at least a foot shorter than him, and it looked like her hands could barely reach each other, but somehow her fingers interlocked, and she began to pump her arms. The entire bar stood still, all of us holding our collective breath.

Pump, pump, pump. Nothing.
You could've heard a pin drop anywhere within a mile.

Pump, pump, pump. Nothing.
I wondered if anyone had called the paramedics.

Pump, pump, pump. Nothing.
Chip's daughter fell to her knees, wailing, begging the universe to be merciful.

Pump, pump, pump. Nothing.
I wanted to scream and run out the door. I closed my eyes, unwilling to face my grandfather's death through this stranger.

Pump, pump, pump.
With my face buried in my hands, I heard the wet pop of a grape or an olive being dislodged from Chip's throat and the vomit that came with it. After more than two full minutes without air, he started breathing again. The whole bar erupted in applause. A collective release of the tension, as we all cheered the nurse and Chip. I looked up just in time to see him being lowered to the ground to recover, his head laying in his daughter's lap. He was mostly unresponsive still, but

she was moaning, stroking his head. I couldn't hear her over all the people praising the nurse, but I could see what she was saying.

"I'm sorry, Dad. I'm so sorry. I love you."

Everything was suddenly overwhelming. It was becoming hard to breathe. A front-row seat for two brushes with death in one night - I had passed my breaking point. I wanted to get out of there as fast as I could. I re-looked at the menu and calculated the total for my order: $23 or so. The food hadn't even been brought to my booth, but I wouldn't have been able to eat anyway. I found a twenty and a ten in my wallet and left them on the table, then I slid out of my booth and headed for the door.

Averting my eyes from the scene around Chip and his daughter, I squeezed past the crowd of onlookers and those discussing what they just witnessed. I stared at the door with every step, my blurry vision informing me that I was crying. A few feet before I reached the exit, the door flung open and flashing red lights flooded the bar. I found myself shoved up against a high-top table as I watched four EMT's push through the crowd, escorting a stretcher. I wondered if these were the same first-responders I encountered in the road less than an hour ago. If this was the same stretcher that carried Gary.

After a few moments of pushing the unlock button on the car's remote key and searching for the blinking taillights, I found my car. It was completely dark out now and I had no idea which way to go, but it didn't matter. I knew what I needed to do, I just wanted to drive for a little while first. I pulled out of my spot and onto the road, heading wherever it took me. My tears became outright sobs. A cathartic release of all the tension and emotion of witnessing two near-death experiences.

After twenty minutes of wandering, I pulled off the road and into an empty grocery store parking lot. I wiped my eyes, steadied my voice, and dug my phone out of my pocket.

My dad picked up after the second ring.

PART 2 - EARTH

196,900,000 square miles of rock, water, and mineral,
Shifting, reacting, reflecting, making habitats habitable,
3,040,000,000,000 trees shading, housing, photosynthesizing,
1,187,049 mountains towering, beautifying, guarding,
Every inch of this planet has the ability to amaze.

7,862,674,000 humans traversing the globe,
Loving, bullying, leaving, wanting one another.
12,775,000 prefixes, pronouns, prepositions heard per year,
Thrilling, scaring, changing us. Re-defining us,
Syllable by syllable, story by story.

31,536,000 micro-experiences piecing together each year,
Breaths, blinks, seconds that fly by or crawl.
22,568,000 wonderings, reactions, fears filling each decade,
Synapses firing, lighting up a map with every thought,
Symphonies and harmonies between world and brain.

30,000,000,000 cells doing the jobs they're shaped for,
Learning, moving, communicating, working together.
3,000,000,000 pairs of adenine, thymine, guanine, and cytosine,
Designing a distinct DNA for each one of us,
Though still 99.9% the same as everyone else's.

Our uniqueness is in a dance with external forces,
With other organisms, experiences, storytellers,
With moments, memories, myths,
Shaping and reshaping us into what we are,
Into the gloriously interesting ones we become.

SECRETS

December 23rd, 4:43PM (24 Hours Before)

Tim Jones, Jr. (Timmy)

With his forehead resting against the glass, Timmy sat in a rear-facing window seat on the Amtrak 283 and watched the snow-covered scenery float away from him. His long, slender body was draped over the seat, with his shoeless feet wedged between the cushion and the frame of the seat facing him. As his forehead started to feel raw, he pulled away from the window and took in his reflection, searching for a look of tranquility or confidence. Instead, he saw angst.

Timmy's nose was long, but not too long, mirroring his entire frame. Deep brown eyes accented his perfectly symmetrical face, which, aside from the red blotch on his forehead from the window, had no blemishes whatsoever. Thick, almost black hair swept across his forehead, creeping over his eyebrows - getting a little long if you ask him, but the length that Phillip likes. At six feet, four inches, Timmy got double-takes everywhere he went. Sometimes, it was because he towered above everyone, and other times just because he was beautiful. He tried to ignore the attention as best as he could, but when you're that tall, you see everything. And every time he felt a pair of eyes on him, his cheeks would flush, his hands would sweat, and he would feel the most powerful pull to run and hide. He was terrified of being seen. Being noticed. Every minute of every day, no matter what he was doing, Timmy felt like he was about to be caught. Like he was in trouble.

"Why can't everyone just leave me alone... let me live my life without someone watching my every move," he would ask Phillip on more than one occasion.

"They notice you because you look like the one person God made without any mistakes. You're too perfect." His flattery fell on deaf ears.

His therapist seemed to think it had to do with growing up in a minister's home. Something about a fishbowl. And maybe because he hadn't yet come out to his family. He hadn't told anyone back home that Phillip was more than just his roommate.

The trees and hillsides backing away from him started to look familiar, telling him they were getting close. He'd spent the four hours since they boarded at Penn Station pretending they were going somewhere else. Allowing the surreality to comfort him. Phillip had fallen asleep just outside Albany, but as they approached Utica it was getting difficult for Timmy to breathe. He needed some reassurance.

"Hey, love," he half whispered, reaching across the gap and gently squeezing just above Phillip's knee to wake him up. "Are we absolutely sure about this?"

Phillip rubbed his eyes and stretched his arms above his head, showing just enough of his ultra-toned six pack to make Timmy smile. He loved how much Phillip cared about his health and fitness, and not only because of how sexy he looked.

"Are we almost there?" Phillip raised his eyebrows and gave a partial smile, pretending to be wide awake.

"Yeah, probably ten minutes." Then, after a slight pause, he added, "I'm not so sure about this."

"About coming out to your family? About telling them that we're engaged? Or about getting married to this piece of Egyptian-American perfection?"

Timmy let out a chuckle. "This piece of perfection might want to wipe the drool off his chin before walking the isle."

"Whatever, you know you can't resist me." Phillip switched sides to sit next to him, putting his hand on Timmy's left thigh.

"No argument here," he said as Phillip leaned in and kissed him.

"You have nothing to worry about, babe. Remember when we told *my* folks?"

"Like I've told you," he replied, leaning back to make sure

he had Phillip's attention, "my parents aren't like yours. Miriam and Randy might be liberal, all-accepting Seattle-ites; but, this week with my mom and dad, you're about to go back to a different century!"

"Timmy," Phillip said, reassuring him, "we're going to get through this week, no matter what. Plus, I know your family is a little behind the times and all, but they've always been really nice and welcoming to me. How bad can it be?"

"With my dad, there's no telling. You know he still scares me."

Timmy thought back on his dad's reactions to things far less controversial. Stomping out of a restaurant because he ordered a chardonnay. Practically disowning Timmy when he voted democrat six years ago. There was no telling how his dad would react to his youngest child being gay. Timmy's thoughts ran wild for a moment.

There's no way he would try to murder me, right? I'm not putting my fiancé's life at risk here, am I? Back in Bible times they would stone a disobedient son, and Dad has a pretty good arm. I can see it now... "Hey Dad, I need to tell you something - I'm gay." "The wind up, and the pitch... Oh! He hits Tim, Jr., right in the face with a ninety-five mile-an-hour fastball. And look, he's grabbing another rock!"

"Plus," Phillip added, bringing Timmy back from his runaway train of thought, "I'm guessing they already know, or at least I think your mom knows. All the times we've visited over the last two years, there's no way she didn't pick up on something in there. In fact, our first time doing it in your childhood bed... your mom totally heard us."

"What?! How do you know? And why are you just saying this now?!"

"I'm telling you; I think she heard us. Or if she didn't hear us, she knew what we were doing."

"I don't believe it."

"Well either way," Phillip said, "I don't think it'll be a huge surprise to either of them."

"Surprise or no surprise, my dad is going to lose his mind."

"I know, babe. You're right. I'm sorry." Phillip pulled Timmy closer and leaned in, but Tim, too weighed down with worry, gave him a quick peck on the forehead and turned back to the window. As the brakes squealed and the Union Station platform burst into view, he felt petrified. Unable to move, as if his body was trying to keep him on the train and away from Utica.

Tim Jones, Sr.

Looking over the meeting agenda in front of him made him feel sick. How had it come to this? He had given everything to this place for almost thirty-eight years, and yet First Congregational Church was shriveling. The budget was hidden away on the second page, but you could see the bold, red ink peeking through. The numbers were like disciplinarians, pointing their fingers and rolling their eyes in disapproval. This elder meeting had now droned on for thirty-five minutes, all of which were spent worrying about paying next month's bills. Tim sat in silence. It took every ounce of his self-control not to confront the three out of five men in the room who weren't tithing. He had looked at the reports just last week, in a moment of desperation. Going two months without paychecks will do that to you.

What was he doing wrong? It wasn't that he was expecting to get rich in this profession, he knew better than that. But still, it was getting tougher and tougher to get up and preach about God's provision while families were leaving, offering plates were mostly empty, and their only pianist was quitting. He wasn't sure how much longer he could last, and his charade of confidence was going to get a lot more complicated starting tonight, because all three kids were coming home.

It had been years since the whole family had been together, back home in Utica. Tim wasn't sure he was ready for them to come sit in the front row for a service. To get a good view of the decay. They had grown up in this church. All of their friendships had been formed here. They were so connected to everything - at least, they *had* been. But it wasn't the sad shape of the church he was worried about most. Tim was trying to ignore the growing whispers of fear and shame stirring in his gut. The inevitable realization that, while he was starting to lose his church, he had already lost his family.

Mary, his oldest, had moved to Rochester two years earlier, and had closed herself off from him. She ignored his calls and rarely returned text messages. Tim had to rely on his wife, Linda, for news about Mary's life. It was even worse with his middle child. Six years ago, Peter had resigned as Tim's assistant pastor, given up Christianity, and announced he was moving to Los Angeles. They'd barely spoken since.

And Tim, Jr., his youngest child, was just so different from the man he was named after. Tim always blamed himself for their lack of connection, yet he felt helpless to do anything about it. He had tried sports. The Syracuse basketball team. The New York Mets. He had tried history. World War Two. Ancient Rome. Nothing worked. Timmy bonded with Linda, instead. Cooking together. Playing card games. Reading fiction.

Somewhere along the way, the wheels had come off the Jones family wagon, and he wasn't sure when or where. He worked hard to set a good example for them. He read them the Bible stories over and over. He prayed for them. But all three of his kids seemed to have forgotten the stories. Ignored his example. Drifted away.

A glint of sunlight drew his attention to the sanctuary. Only a narrow portion was visible to him out the window in the conference room's door. A stained-glass depiction of Jesus holding a shepherd's crook was glowing orange from the sunset outside. He remembered his first day as Pastor, kneeling in front of that window.

March 1st, 1983, 6:15am

Only a few weeks beyond his twenty-eighth birthday, Tim was shaking as he unlocked the church's front doors. He went straight to the sanctuary and began walking through the rows, his left hand instinctively following the grooves worn into the oak pews. The prick of a splinter drew a little blood at the base of his index finger, and he thought of the irony of

101

shedding blood in front of stained-glass Jesus. In just a few short hours, he would preach his first sermon in front of the congregation. This was the day he'd been dreaming of for so long, and he was going to do it right. He'd reviewed and re-reviewed his sermon so many times, his notes were almost ruined.

The passage: Abraham and Sarah

The main point: "If you are faithful to God, he will see you through"

Today marked the beginning of his leg of the race. He would remain faithful to the truth, raise up God-fearing children, save souls, and warn against the evils of the world. And, by so doing, he'd solidify his spot as one of God's faithful men. He had no doubt that God would see him through. It didn't matter what anyone else thought or did, he would live a life worthy of respect and honor. He knelt in front of the giant stained-glass window to say a quick prayer, before heading to his study to go over his notes one last time.

Everyone was looking at him expectantly. What did he miss?

"How do you think we should handle it, Pastor Jones?" Ed Nantz followed up his question by clicking his pen three times, ready to record Tim's answer verbatim.

"Handle what?"

"Miss Serdahl's request for financial support."

"Oh, right." They had reached the final agenda item for today's meeting and, even though each man had a vote, in reality the elders always followed Tim's lead.

"Well, we do have a mandate to care for the needy, and Jessica is a single mother," he began. All five heads nodded in unison. "But we also cannot compromise on sexual immorality. Jessica had her daughter out of wedlock and has refused to ever admit wrongdoing, even as many of our church members have showed her hospitality and compassion. Compromise is a slippery slope. If we bend on our convictions even once, it becomes very difficult to regain our standards." He was a steam engine, gathering speed as it rolled downhill, leading to the grand pronouncement. "And, seeing as how she's not an official member, I don't think we have a choice. The compassion fund has been set up specifically for church members in need."

Bill Dawson, the compassionate one, stammered through a suggestion.

"Perhaps we could, uh, given her situation being hospitalized and everything, organize something less official for those who might want to contribute to her bills?"

Tim paused to think. It angered him that his church members would want to pay for this woman's hospital bills instead of giving to the church, but this situation was complicated.

Jessica Serdahl had been coming to First Congregational Church ever since she was sixteen - right after her parents' accident - and was well-liked by everyone. But later, as a single twenty-one-year-old, she became pregnant. Since she refused to tell anyone who the father was, or admit the sin she'd committed, she wasn't able to officially join the church. And yet, she had the audacity to continue attending. And when her daughter, Alethea, was born, it was as if everyone except Tim decided to forget about the whole thing. Tim's wife, Linda, was especially fond of Alethea and always defended Jessica when she came up in conversation at home. He knew that he would have a hard time explaining any inaction right now, especially to his wife. Linda had even offered to have Alethea stay with them while her mom was in the hospital.

"Bill makes a good point," he said, "while we can't use church funds directly, I'm sure there are several people who would be willing to show mercy on her. Especially during the Christmas season."

As the meeting ended, Tim slowly walked down the hallway to his study, his feet landing heavily on the tattered, beige carpet. He tossed the papers from the meeting onto his desk and sunk into his brown leather chair, letting his momentum spin him so he was looking out his window at the bare maple tree, clothed in ice. He tried to think of a plan. He wanted to be strong. He wanted to put on a brave face. To convince the elders and the congregation that things would be fine. The only problem was, he needed to convince himself first.

The warm hum of his vibrating cell phone eased his thoughts away from the church. Linda's blue eyes stared at him from the caller-ID, making him feel exposed. Almost by instinct, he grabbed a book from the edge of his desk and laid it on top of the meeting notes, shielding the budget from view. He hesitated for a moment, holding his finger above the screen, trying to figure out when this picture was taken. Something about it mesmerized him. It was the camera angle, maybe. Or the way her ocean-colored dress hugged her shoulders and the creases around her eyes made you feel like you were the only two people in the world. Like you shared a secret.

I wish she would still look at me like that... when was that from, anyway?

His index finger sent Linda's face back into oblivion, exchanging it for her voice.

"...And please don't be late this time," were the first words he heard. Linda had this habit of getting through an entire paragraph before you could get the phone to your ear.

"Linda," he interrupted, "when is the photo on my phone from?"

"What photo on your phone?"

"You're wearing that blue dress you used to have, and I think we were downstairs in the church basement?"

"I don't know, Tim. I didn't think you knew how to put pictures on your phone. Anyway, listen, Pete and Eyana land in Syracuse at 6:39PM ok? Can you please be there on time for once? And don't get into it with him on the drive home. I told them they can sleep in Pete's old room, and I don't want you to fight with him about it. Eyana shouldn't have to sit through one of your arguments."

Eyana?! You're worried about Eyana? Our son is living in sin with a liberal atheist, who is coming into my house for a week, not to mention that you are letting them sleep together! An unmarried couple, sleeping

105

together, under my roof, and you drop this news on me today, when it's too late to do anything about it. As if I don't know what you're doing… and yet, instead of supporting me, you're worried about offending Eyana!?

"Don't worry, Hun, I'll be nice. I know how important this week is to you."

There was a brief silence, making Tim wonder if he had accidentally said his thoughts out loud.

He added, "…And to me, I mean. This week is important to all of us."

"I just miss the old times, Tim," she replied thinly, "it's been so long since we've all been together under one roof. We need some good family time."

Is she crying?

"I know, you're right." He was trying to sound strong, now. "This week is going to be good for us. For all of us. Our kids can use some time back home, away from all the distractions and temptations, and around good values and helpful reminders. You know, I might even get to have some good heart-to-heart chats with each of them, too!"

Linda didn't sound convinced. "I just want us to all get along. It is Christmas, you know, Tim? I don't think a little peace on earth is too much to ask for. No arguments about the Bible or fights about politics or any of that. As a mother, I just miss being a family… especially this time of year."

Tim settled himself and agreed. "Sounds good, Lind." Then, not wanting to end on such a downer, he offered more clues to his photo-puzzle. "You were wearing pearls and Brenda Pierce is in the background."

"What are you talking about?"

"The photo! You know, on my phone?!"

"What about it?"

"Do you know when it was taken? Blue dress, pearls, Brenda…?"

Linda mumbled a few unintelligible syllables like a mathematician doing long division. Then, she announced, "Our twenty-fifth anniversary party, New Year's Eve, 2003."

Tim knew she added the date in order to remind him that their anniversary was in eight days. It was their fortieth this year, which made it easier for her to convince all the kids to come home. He didn't have anything big planned. Getting the family together was all that Linda really wanted, anyway. And besides, celebrating just didn't feel genuine anymore. It wasn't like his phone's picture. Back then, they were happy. They were in love. Their kids hadn't fallen off the deep end yet and the church was doing well. Life was simple. But now, the wrinkles around their eyes were signs of stress and heartache, not creases of joy.

"Wow," he half-whispered, "that long ago, huh? Seems like a different lifetime! Back before…"

"Before what?" Her question caught him off guard.

What do you want me to say? Back before our one son chose you over me, my other son betrayed me, our daughter started running around with every guy in Rochester, and no one had enough respect for their father to remain faithful?!

"Just back when our family felt closer… back before they all grew up and left the house, I guess."

"I miss those days too, Tim," she said between sniffles.

"I know, Lind." His reply sounded stiff, like a news anchor signing off.

The line went dead. As he pulled his phone away from his face, it reverted to dutifully displaying the time: 5:23pm. He shoved the documents into his briefcase, threw on his jacket, and scooped up his keys. He had to get going if he was going to make it to the airport in time.

Linda Jones

Her husband's voice was so loud, Linda's body was rattling with each syllable. She was pushing buttons on the dashboard, trying to turn him down, but all she managed to do was reduce the treble in the speakers, making him sound like Darth Vader.

Ugh, this is impossible! Why did I ever let Mary set this car-phone thing up in the first place. I just wanted to talk on the phone! It's hard enough to drive in the snow, with Alethea in the backseat. I don't need Tim screaming at me while I'm doing it. And what is he droning on about anyway…? Is he still talking about the picture on his phone?

Finally, her frantic button-pushing worked, and his voice returned to a normal volume, albeit still in a lower range than normal. She was trying to make the drive from their home way out on Edgewood Street to the Utica train station, while snow was starting to fall, and it was not the easiest task to pull off. She needed to give the reminder quickly, get off the phone, and focus on the roads.

"Ok, Listen Tim," she interrupted, "Just don't forget to pick up Pete and Eyana, ok? 6:13PM at Hancock in Syracuse. Got it?"

"Yes, yes, Linda." She could hear Tim rolling his eyes. "Just tell me when this photo is from…?!"

"It's from our twenty-fifth anniversary party, New Year's Eve, 2003."

Linda hated New Year's Eve. Partly because it was their anniversary. A day to celebrate their marriage, which for the last several years had been an unhappy one. Also, because it was a day to be with loved ones and ring in a new twelve months with hope and joy, but all her loved ones had been pushed away by their father. So much so, that they hadn't even been all together as a family for six years and hadn't been together as a *happy* family for more like ten or twelve. But she also hated December thirty-first because it was a reminder of New Year's Eve, 1977. The one night that set her down a path of misery and heartache so strong she still felt pain thinking about it, forty-one years later. At least this year she would have her kids with her. She could put her mind and body to work as a mother and be at peace. That is, as long as Tim didn't cause too much strife.

"There's one more thing," she said, trying to sound authoritative, "I told Pete that the two of them can sleep in Pete's room."

"What?" Tim protested.

"Tim," she sang in a disciplinary tone, "I don't want you to get into it with him. This week is about one thing: peace. I haven't had my kids home in years and all I'm asking for is a calm, happy visit. This is really important to me." She could feel the tears welling up in her eyes. "Consider it your anniversary gift to me. No arguments. No home-sermons. No fights."

Tim was silent. Linda wondered if she had come on too strong. It was just that she had been looking forward to this week for so long, hoping that it might spark something in him. Maybe he'd miss the kids so much that seeing them all together would soften him. Bring him back from his obsession with the church and his reputation as its pastor. Or maybe he would at least want to impress the children. Set an example by proving to them that he was madly in love with his wife of forty years. But instead, he seemed more distracted than ever. More concerned with the church, or his home projects, or God knows what else. She tried one more time.

"I just miss the old times, Tim," she said with a quivering bottom lip, "It's been so long since we've all been together under one roof and really felt like a family, you know?"

"Yeah," he said, distracted.

She wondered if he was still looking at his phone. "I just wish we could go back to the way things were before. Back to how it felt in that picture on your phone."

"That was a different time, Lind, back before…" His voice trailed off.

Yeah, it was different, alright! Back before you decided that your career was more important than your family! Back before you started driving our kids away, by pressuring them to be what you wanted and by your obnoxious need to be right all the time!

"Before what?" she snapped, hoping her question didn't sound too much like a cross-examiner going for the confession.

"Just back when things were simple. Back when the church was thriving, and our family felt closer. Before the kids all grew up and started drifting away, I guess."

Just as I thought. All you care about is whether or not people listen to you and respect you. That's what this week is to you, isn't it?! You want Pete to come back, crawling on all fours, begging for forgiveness. You think Timmy will just magically change his interests around to be more like you. And what? Are you going to corner Mary and interrogate her? Give her a lecture about purity!?

Linda realized she was crying and pulled over to the side of the road, hanging up the phone. She knew she'd never be able to say her honest thoughts out loud to him. She felt trapped. What choice did she have but to carry on? To smile and play the part of a happy pastor's wife? She looked at Alethea through the rear-view mirror. She was looking out the window at the snow-covered houses, oblivious to Linda and her phone call. For a brief moment, she daydreamed that she had adopted Alethea. That she had a five-year-old in the house again. That her life had meaning again.

December 23rd, 5:29PM (23 Hours Before)

Mary Jones

Mary moved her fork aimlessly around the now-empty dessert plate. Brian, or Ben, or Bryce - she couldn't remember his name - was still droning on about his job as an accountant, or purchaser, or underwriter. Meanwhile, she tried to ignore her growing concern about her period being five days late. She was never late.

Byron, or Bobby, was making this one of the more boring dates she'd had in a long time, and to make matters worse, she couldn't drink too much. There was still the two-hour drive to Utica tonight. At least she had her dessert, though, a Raspberry Walnut Torte. Mary always ordered dessert, even if she was paying. She considered it her insurance policy for the date. If it was really dull, or if he was an under-performer in bed… at least she got something tasty out of it!

Or maybe, rather than insurance, it was her reward for the hellish regiment she put herself through for these outings. Strict diets, regular workouts and Pilates, the process to get the dress on and looking good. Not to mention the uncomfortable but sexy undergarments, the makeup and hair, the painful shoes and prepping of the apartment. And don't forget the Uber ride across town and dealing with the snow. It was a lot, and she owed herself these small moments of tastebud euphoria.

Come on, already! Who taught you how to date…? Stop talking and ask for the check. You may be gorgeous, but I do not have time to hear about your stupid pet rabbit, or whatever!

She had learned the subtleties to watch for. The fortune-tellers of the date. The angle of the hips when talking about something personal. If he makes eye contact, looks away, or looks her over. The assertiveness to pay for the meal or the awkward moment when someone suggests they split the check. And the most telling of all: his reaction to her move. She couldn't stand to hear another story, so she waited for him to take a breath, and pounced.

Over years of practice, Mary had perfected the move. It was in the way she leaned forward, ever so slightly, revealing and concealing at the same time. And in her half-smile, curling her upper lip in a way that made him feel like they had shared an inside joke. And you can't forget the eyebrows, raised about halfway, slightly more on the inside than the outside, melting his confidence while inviting him closer. With impeccable timing, Mary slid her hand over Blaine's, or Baldwin's, with the lightest of caresses, letting her pointer finger slip under his pinkie, asking the question:

"So… what should we do next…?"

And then came the closers. After the lean and smile to set it up, and after touching the hand and the question to get his attention, the real secret to the move was in Mary's eyes. She had big, baby-blue eyes. The kind that could sink into you and make you forget everything else, and she knew how to use them. At five-feet-eleven, with toned legs, wearing her deep V-neck black dress and a 32D push up bra, and her thick, disheveled brown hair that laid over her shoulders, Mary looked stunning. She was difficult to ignore in any situation, but once you were sitting across from her, within striking distance of her eyes, resistance was impossible. Her move worked every time. The power dynamics would shift drastically, and the next few minutes would unfold as if from a script.

Brad, or Brandon, would stutter and start to laugh nervously, eventually getting out the word "well," half as a question, and half the start of a sentence he was struggling to form.

Mary would then say, "how about we start by going back to my place and we can take it from there?"

"Sure," he would reply, "that, uh, sounds great." His nerves would cause him to (a) spill his drink, (b) overpay by at least $20, or (c) trip over his own shoes. But, before you knew it, they'd be making out in the Uber, up in her apartment for whatever sort of sex she was in the mood for, and then he'd be back out the door and headed home with only a fuzzy memory of the whole night.

Occasionally, there'd be a second date. Never a third. Mary wasn't looking for a relationship. She was a free spirit, enjoying the independence of only having to worry about herself. She wanted control. She avoided vulnerability. This was *her* life, and she wasn't ready to share it. To be responsible for someone else's wellbeing.

As they waited for their ride, outside in the cold, Brody, or Butch, began to shiver. "I hate Rochester in the winter," he said.

Mary wasn't listening. She was reading a text from her dad.

Hey Mary, headed to Syracuse to pick up Pete.
Have you left yet? Storm is supposed to get worse tonight.
I'll call you in a bit.
-Dad

Checking the weather on her phone, she saw he was right. She was going to have to wrap up this date early. She opened the car door and turned around, keeping her body in the opening, and quickly excused herself to Brenden, or Barney.

"I'm really sorry, but I have to go. I have to drive to Utica tonight before the snow gets worse. Can we do this again after I'm back? I had a really great time!"

The thud of her door, closing her off from the outside, drowned out his confused response. She let her head fall back against the seat and closed her eyes, already moving on from Braylon, or Beck...

Linda

Linda's fingers tightened around the steering wheel as she turned onto Main Street. The streetlights that lined this part of town were starting to blink on, as the sunlight faded. She was having a hard time seeing the road, but she couldn't tell if the blurriness was from her tears or because her wipers weren't keeping up with the falling snow. The flakes that were coming down were microscopic, looking more like dust than precipitation. The kind of snow that coated all the deck furniture in that thin, sparkling blanket that made you want to sip hot cocoa and stare out the window for an entire afternoon.

The only problem was that it was also the kind of snow that was falling in Albany on February 23rd, 1978, which was the day that Linda had spent almost forty-one years trying to heal from. It was amazing how much one day had defined her life, even though it was all hidden away. She hadn't told anyone about that day. Not her parents, not her husband Tim, not even her best friend Genie.

She was searching for something to get her mind off that awful memory, when she passed Adrian Drive, where Jessica Serdahl's house was. A small beige ranch, with large bushes protecting the living room windows and an old basketball hoop in the driveway that looked like it might fall over at any moment. The whole property was disheveled and overgrown. The result of Jess being a single mother, working two jobs, and living in an inherited home she didn't have time to manage.

She often felt motherly instincts whenever Jess came up in conversation, wanting to protect her from anyone trying to disparage her. The poor girl lost her entire family before her seventeenth birthday, has been raising Alethea on her own, and now she was stuck in the hospital with no way to pay the bills.

"What is she supposed to do?" she had asked Tim the other night as she was finishing up the dishes, "raise her daughter on her own? Deal with cancer on her own?"

"What she is supposed to do," he snapped back with the pompous air of a judge pronouncing a sentence, "is work hard to provide for Alethea, raise her to be a good Christian, and be grateful for all the support she's received over the years, despite her promiscuity!"

"That's rich, coming from you!" Linda could feel herself losing control. She dropped the spoon she was holding into the sink and paused to dry off her hands. "Men never have to deal with the consequences. I don't see anyone holding a rock, ready to stone whoever Alethea's father is! You men are always ready to have sex, but never ready to take responsibility for your actions!"

"That's exactly what I'm doing - taking my responsibility seriously as the pastor of this church. A church that she's not even a member of."

"As if that's her fault!? She's not a member because all the 'perfect' men in charge won't let her join! It was six years ago, Tim! What do you want her to do? Get on her knees and beg for forgiveness that she had sex before marriage?! Of all people, I expected *you* to have more compassion!"

"Why are you always coming to her defense, Lind? Why don't you ever support me? Consider my side on things?"

"Gee, I don't know Tim!" She turned back to the sink, plunging her hands into the warm soapy water. She wasn't sure where this anger was coming from, but her jaw clenched and her forehead was sweating. She knew she should have stopped there, but she couldn't help herself.

"And one more thing... Alethea is going to be staying with us until she's out of the hospital, so you better watch what you say. You'll have to dig deep and find some self-control this week, instead of running your mouth about every person in the church." She was almost screaming now.

"If you dare talk badly about Jess in front of her daughter, so help me…" She was interrupted by the slamming of the front door. Tim had heard enough and stormed out.

Linda had spent the next two days preparing the house for Alethea, and for her own kids to come home, while barely exchanging words with Tim. That was partly why the phone call had bothered her so much. They had been in a lifeless marriage for a few years now, yet he had never once admitted that anything was wrong. She didn't need him to have all the solutions or to transform overnight, she just wanted him to say some combination of words that signaled his awareness of the problem. He never complained about their relationship or indicated that he wished they were closer. He complained about the church. He complained about the government. Just once, Linda wanted him to complain about her. Did he even care that they had stopped loving each other?

Checking on Alethea in the backseat, she felt a rush of compassion. She wondered if this was what grandmothers felt. As they eased to a stop for a red light, Linda thought about Alethea's grandma, and how she never got to meet her granddaughter. She also thought about what it would've been like to be Jessica's mom through all this.

The silver lining with Jessica, though, is that her mother isn't around anymore to go through this. Is it wrong of me to think like that? That her mother is better off dead than having to deal with the way her daughter has been treated for getting pregnant without a husband? Having to look people in the eye, feeling the stares from everyone at church. I can't imagine going through something like this as a mother. Tim would probably have to resign. I mean, think of the Harrisons! Who could've seen that coming!? James coming out as gay like that? That was it, right? He became gay...? Or was it queer...?

The memory of her baby, Tim, Jr., sneaking a kiss with his friend Phillip in her kitchen last summer snuck up on her. She knew he had always been attracted to boys, and that he and Phillip were more than just friends. In fact, she knew all about everything with Timmy, deep down, but she kept it hidden, even from herself. It was easier to pretend that he was going through a phase, or that he was just experimenting. Someday she'd have to confront the reality of her youngest child's lifestyle, but it was too terrifying to worry about for now. Not this week, when she finally had her whole family back together. Maybe, if she ignored it, the whole situation would just go away somehow. Of course, Linda knew better than anyone that difficult things like this don't just go away, but she needed to hold out hope. Hope of finding a way to protect Timmy from his father. Tim could never find out. It would kill him. Or, if not, he might kill his son, and Linda would do anything to protect her children.

"Pay attention, Linda," she said out loud to herself, "the light is green and you're going to be late!"

December 23rd, 6:13PM (22 Hours Before)

Pete Jones

The flight attendant's scratchy voice interrupted Pete's train of thought and reminded him that he was about to be back in the worst place on earth: Utica, New York. "We are now making our final descent. Please make sure your seat back and tray table are returned to their full upright position, and that all large electronics are powered off and stowed."

Pete clicked save, gently closed the lid to his laptop, and wedged it between the novels in his backpack. The capstone paragraph of this barely adequate blog post would have to wait. He turned to look at his girlfriend, Eyana, who was staring out her window into the darkness. Pete was glad to let her have the window seat. The lights of Syracuse below would just remind him of the last time he was at Hancock International, almost six years ago, when he ran away from everything in Utica. His family. His job as assistant pastor. The woman he loved.

It took Pete almost two years to get over that heartbreak. For the first several months in L.A., he had regular panic attacks, a lingering depression, and no interest in dating women. In fact, Eyana was his first relationship since leaving New York state. They'd been together for almost two years and things were going well, but to him everything still felt fragile. Like one bad night and he'd be single again. No matter how happy she made him or how much he trusted her, Pete knew that as soon as they took their relationship to the next level, Eyana would change her mind about him and be out the door, leaving his heart in pieces. Better safe than alone. He'd been betrayed enough times. Hurt by enough people. Pete had learned to protect himself.

Sitting back in his seat, Pete looked over at his girlfriend and wondered if they'd made a mistake. Bringing Eyana home to meet his family was a big step, and he had no clue what he was getting her into. Maybe this was too much.

He slid his left hand into hers and she looked over at him, causing him to smile. There was something about her face that soothed him. Her light brown skin had a warm glow to it and the whites of her narrow eyes were luminous against her coffee-colored irises. She looked sophisticated and powerful, and every time Pete looked at her, he was reminded that she was out of his league. That every day with her brought him closer to the inevitable breakup and ensuing loneliness.

As the flight attendants made their final pass through the aisles, Pete looked over at the seven-year-old boy sitting across from him. He and Eyana had begun talking about serious things like moving in together, having kids, and their beliefs about marriage, but every time they'd discuss it, Pete would cut off the conversation before it got too serious, afraid of being hurt again. He was having trouble sleeping from the stress. In his nightmares, he would ask Eyana to move in together, but she would shape-shift into Jess Serdahl and the furniture would re-arrange itself into his parents' house in Utica. As the floor would crack open, Pete would reach out to Eyana/Jess, trying to avoid falling into the abyss. Trying to be together. But she would put two hands on his chest and shove him backward, sending him tumbling into the vortex, and Pete would wake up screaming and sweating.

"You ok?" Eyana asked, as the plane banked left, lining up with the runway.

"I hope so," he offered, resting his head on her shoulder, "or at least I will be if we survive this week." He was thinking about his dad. Tim had taken Pete's resignation pretty hard six years ago, and they had never worked through it. And besides that, Pete knew his dad would have a hard time with him bringing Eyana home.

When they had booked their tickets a month earlier, Pete had called Linda to tell her he was coming home. She was ecstatic. She cried tears of joy as she listed off items to bring and meals she was planning. And his mom assured him that they didn't need to get a hotel, because she would "take care of" Dad's insistence that he and Eyana sleep in separate rooms. Pete was confident that "taking care of it" meant not telling Dad anything, until it was too late.

"I know you don't want to be here," Eyana said, "but I'm looking forward to it. I think it'll be good for us - me meeting your family and seeing all the places from your childhood."

"You think that now," he quipped, "but just wait! These people are insane. And my childhood is something I'm trying to forget, not relive. Why do you think I haven't come back here in so long?!"

As the plane bounced onto the tarmac, he pulled his phone out of his pocket and turned it on, trying to see if he had any messages after eight hours of plane rides. The phone lit up and showed the local time: 6:18PM. They had landed right on time.

December 24th, 7:24AM (9 Hours Before)

Tim, Jr. (Timmy)

Timmy slipped out from under the handmade quilt on his childhood bed, making sure not to wake Phillip. He'd been awake for almost an hour already, unable to settle his running mind. As his arms matched his brain, rapidly rummaging through his suitcase to find an outfit for the day, he kept simulating the dreaded moment planned for this week. Practicing coming out to his dad. Every time he ran the simulation, no matter how he approached the conversation, it ended in disaster. There was no way around it and Timmy was terrified.

He paused at the bedroom door and watched his fiancé sleep, wishing the serenity on Phillip's face were contagious, then he slipped out into the hallway and grabbed a towel for his shower from the linen closet. He smiled at Mary, who was coming out of the bathroom as he was going in, but she didn't smile back. She looked miserable. Like she hadn't slept all night. Timmy watched her zombie-walk back into her bedroom and then spent his entire shower worrying about his sister. She seemed fine last night when she got in from Rochester, but he wondered what might have happened after he went to bed.

The house was empty and quiet as he came downstairs to make some breakfast, other than the sound of a drawer closing in the kitchen. Probably his mom getting started on the eggs. But, as he made the U-turn at the base of the stairs to face the doorway into the kitchen, Timmy's throat dried up. The drawer sound was made by his father, who was standing against the counter, all alone in the kitchen, drinking from a mug.

You'll be fine. It'll be fine. Just walk in there and start scrambling some eggs. Nothing is going to happen. He can't figure out your secret by the way you make breakfast. One foot in front of the other.

"Morning," his dad grumbled, looking up just long enough for Timmy to see the dark rings under his eyes. He looked pretty rough as well. Maybe he was up late with Mary? Probably scolding her. Telling her how sinful her lifestyle was. It looked like neither of them got much sleep.

"Hey," he said, "I'm going to make some eggs. Do you want some?" He grabbed the frying pan from the drawer under the oven, noticing the out-of-place bottle of Tylenol on the counter, as his dad mumbled something about needing to work on his sermon and shuffled out of the room. He was left alone. He was safe.

After scrambling enough eggs to feed the whole neighborhood, Timmy popped two slices of bread into the toaster and started brewing coffee. Linda would make her entrance any minute now, and the two of them would enjoy the benefits of being the only early-risers in the family.

"The toast is perfect, Hun," Linda said as she made up her plate two minutes later.

"Well, of course it is," he said. "Fortunately, we have identical tastes in breakfast foods." He smiled at his mom joining him at the small bistro table in the kitchen corner. "It's not so easy with Phillip, you know! He prefers eggs over-medium, and he won't even touch toast that--" Timmy caught himself.

He felt blood rush into his cheeks as he tried to contort his face into a look that seemed normal. Composed. Unfazed by the way he was casually describing the intimate details of Phillip's breakfast preferences. He silently chided himself for his error.

He had been lured in by the comforts of familiarity. Breakfast with his mother, in this kitchen, before anyone else was up. Something he'd done hundreds of times. He had let his guard down and came dangerously close to accidentally revealing too much too soon. He quickly shifted topics to discuss their grocery list and Linda shifted with him. They wrote down everything they needed as they finished their breakfasts, and then headed out on their annual trip to the store.

Grocery shopping the morning of Christmas Eve had become a tradition for Linda and Tim, Jr., starting in his early teens, when his mom had forgotten a critical ingredient for their big family dinner. Christmas dinner was the holiest of meals and it had to be perfect, so Linda set off for the store in a mild panic. Always the "momma's boy," Timmy just followed her out of the house and into the car. From that year on, for reasons unknown to him, his mom would always find an excuse to take him grocery shopping for Christmas dinner.

Some years, they would go the twenty-second or twenty-third, but once he'd moved out of the house, Linda started waiting for him to get into town to make her store run. There was no planning. No acknowledgment of the tradition. It was an unspoken ritual, and he loved having his mother all to himself for the few hours.

As they made their way down the frozen foods isle at Price Chopper, he felt like young Timmy again. No bio-tech research job waiting for him in the city. No wedding planning with Phillip. No impending doom on the other side of coming out to his family this week. Just him pushing a cart and his mom filling it with food. He felt secure. Even secure enough to test the waters a little.

"Hey mom…?" he said.

"Hey Timmy…?" she jokingly parroted, adding vanilla ice cream to the cart.

This was a good start. A joking Linda is a happy Linda.

"How's Dad feeling these days?"

"Oh, you know Dad." Linda continued scanning the shelves as she talked. "Same as always, I suppose. He never goes to the doctor unless there's an emergency. And the last emergency was ten or twelve years ago. You were still in school, Dear."

"The kidney stones?"

"Yes," she groaned, trying to reach some apple juice on the top shelf.

"Mom, you're telling me Dad hasn't been to a doctor since I was a junior in high school?!"

Linda gave a slight grunt of affirmation, while she read the nutrition facts on the juice's label.

"Well, that's not good," he said in disbelief, taking a second to shake off the oncoming anxiety about his father's health. "Anyway, I meant Dad's emotional well-being. What's his stress level been lately?"

"His stress level? It's fine. I mean, it's never easy being a pastor and all, but I'd say he's handling things ok. Why?"

Tim Jr. Wondered what "things" were being "handled."

"Because I have some things to share with him this week. Things that might be a… surprise."

His mom put the juice in the cart and turned away. Tim thought he saw the quickest flash of concern on his mom's face, as she grabbed the front of the cart, leading them toward the checkout lanes, and he wondered what it meant. Should he do a test run with his mother? After all, Phillip thinks she already knows. He needed to know what she was thinking. What she would be thinking if she learned what the surprise was.

Before he knew what was happening, his hands were stopping the cart, so she'd pause and turn around, and his lungs were taking a deep breath, preparing to speak. Some part of his brain had taken control of the situation and had decided that Timmy was going to come out to Linda. Right now. Right here. In the chips and snacks isle.

"Mom, I need to tell you something." What was happening? This was not how he had planned to do this. Linda was staring at her youngest child, eyes wide.

"You know that Phillip and I are close, right?"

"Let's check out, Timmy," she whispered.

"No, hold on, Mom. I need to tell you this." Tim Jr took a breath.

Linda kept whispering. "We can talk about this later."

He ignored her. "Basically, the thing is that I'm gay. I'm not straight, Mom. I'm gay. And Phillip… he's gay too. And we've been dating for a few years, actually. We are… well we love each other." He was getting louder and more defensive the longer Linda's face stayed frozen. "And you know what?! We're getting married. Yep. Married. A wedding and the whole thing. So… so… so, yeah. That's what I needed to tell you. And, I guess, what I need to tell Dad. What I'm going to tell Dad this week."

Without saying a word, his mom carried out a military-like about-face and walked briskly to check-out lane four, gripping the cart tightly behind her.

Linda

Her Christmas Eve grocery shopping trip with Timmy was sacred. One of her favorite outings of each year. This year, Linda found herself looking forward to the ritual more than usual. Needing it, even. Perhaps it was because of how rocky things felt with her husband. Or that her entire family was going to be together for the first time in what felt like forever. Whatever the reason, as she walked up and down the isles with her youngest at her side, Linda felt a sense of calm. Safety. Relief.

In here, everything was ok. No unpaid bills to go through. No stressed-out husband to manage. No reminders of ancient, painful memories. She was just a mother, and her precious son was keeping her company. Linda watched Timmy's face as they talked, trying to take a mental snapshot of every expression. Ever since she'd gotten pregnant with Mary, her children had become her reason for living. She would do anything for them. Sacrifice anything or anyone to protect them. But these days, with the kids all out on their own, her life felt as empty as her house. But not this week. This week the house would be bustling. Everyone was back and she was preparing a Christmas dinner. Linda's heart was full once again.

But, as they turned and started down the frozen foods isle, Linda's mom-senses put her on alert. Something had shifted in Timmy. She could tell he had something on his mind, and she had a pretty good guess what that might be. If she was right, he was about to disrupt the peace. A preemptive strike that would surely start a war between her husband and her child.

Linda knew who she would support if lines were being drawn and sides were being chosen. She'd made a vow in 1978, after all. But it didn't need to come to that. She wouldn't let it come to that. She was going to stop this before it could even begin.

She held the apple juice up to her face, pretending to read the label, trying to regain some composure. Then she made a break for the registers, but Timmy stopped the cart. She tried to shout, yell, overtake her son's voice, but all that came out was a faint whisper.

Then Timmy said it. Out loud and outright.

She sent all their chosen groceries down the miniature conveyor belt in silence. She was panicking inside. What was she supposed to say to her son? What would she say to Tim, Sr.? No, nothing would be said to him, under any circumstances. She wasn't ready to lay herself down on the altar just yet. Maybe she could convince Timmy to keep quiet and wait a little longer.

Linda spent the entire drive home giving a fifteen-minute rant about all the things causing stress in her husband's life - church attendance dwindling, having no paychecks for two months, even the strain in their marriage - and why Timmy could not talk about his "homosexual lifestyle" any further this week, no matter what. She was a preacher giving her most passionate sermon. Timmy averted his eyes and stayed silent.

December 24th, 8:54AM (8 Hours Before)

Mary

So far, this had been the worst morning of Mary's life. Stomach pain had woken her at six, and she'd spent most of the time since then sitting on the floor of the upstairs bathroom, leaning over to vomit in the toilet every few minutes. At first, she assumed it was food poisoning and thought back to what she'd eaten on her date last night. Something with chicken. But then, thinking about last night, she remembered excusing herself, heading to the restroom at the back of the restaurant, and checking the calendar on her phone's period-tracking app. Her stomach lurched. She still hadn't gotten her period, and now she was six days late.

Mary knew she needed to take a pregnancy test, yet she stayed glued to the bathroom floor. Unable to will herself into her car and to the store. There were too many obstacles in her way. What if someone asked her where she was going? What if she vomited all over her car's interior? Or on the stairs? Her mind continued its search for excuses to stay, but Mary knew the one question that was at the core of her inability to move: What if she tested positive?

She was not ready to be a mother, and she was really not ready to be a single mother. Her whole life would change and there would be so many things she felt unprepared to deal with. The responsibility. The pressure. The judgment and mistreatment from everyone - especially her own parents. The permanence of it. There's no return policy, you know. If you have a child, you become their mom forever.

As her fears continued to coalesce, Mary decided she would rather know the truth than suffer through constant worry, and she found her chance to head to the store. Her mom and Timmy had just left to go grocery shopping, Pete was still sleeping, and her throw-up had turned to dry-heaving. The perfect window.

She was back home in the bathroom within twenty minutes, unboxing it and reading the directions. It was one of those tests that was in the shape of an exclamation point, matching the urgency she felt. Her hands shaking, she lowered her pants and positioned her body over the toilet, squatting a few inches above the seat.

Halfway through taking the test, Pete knocked on the door. She almost fell over.

"You almost done in there?" Pete yawned.

"Yeah, give me a minute," She hollered, putting the test on the edge of the sink. It needed to sit for a couple minutes, so she fake-flushed the toilet and opened the door for Pete.

It wasn't until she heard the bathroom door close and lock behind her, with Pete inside, that she realized she had left the test in plain sight.

She was terrified enough of the possibility of being pregnant, let alone sharing that potential bombshell of a headline with her younger brother. She rapped on the door. Machine-gun fire rattling out her angst.

"Pete, wait. I need back in."

"What? Hang on a sec."

"No, it's an emergency. I've been sick all morning. Trust me, I need to get in there."

"Ok, ok. I'm coming, just let me-" Pete's voice cut off and there were a few seconds of silence before he opened the door.

Mary's eyes darted to the counter. It was empty. She looked up and saw Pete staring back at her, eyebrows raised, holding the test in his hand.

"It's positive," he said.

Pete

Pete couldn't tell if he was happy for Mary or jealous of her. He also couldn't tell how Mary felt about this news. She was staring at the test in disbelief, sitting on the toilet, lid closed. He tried to fill the silence, telling Mary about how he and Eyana had been discussing moving in together and maybe even having kids.

"You should," she suggested softly, "you'd be a great dad."

"You think so?"

"I know so."

Pete thought about when they were kids. Mary was always standing up for him. Covering for him. Protecting him. She was the strong one; he was needy. She had a plan; he followed her every move. In fact, Pete couldn't remember a time when his sister was vulnerable like this. When she needed *him* to be strong for *her*.

"You know," he tried, attempting to mimic the tone he'd heard her use over the years, "you're going to be a great mom."

"I don't know, Pete," she murmured, "I don't even know who the father is, and I don't know if I can raise a kid by myself."

"You raised me by yourself," he joked, smiling.

"Yeah, and look how you turned out," she shot back.

Pete took hold of her arm and eased her onto her feet, giving her a big hug. Mary rested her chin on his shoulder and let out a sigh. He smiled. It felt good to take care of her, for once.

"Seriously, you are the strongest person I know, Sis. You've got this."

She set the pregnancy test on the counter, right next to a red sparkly child's toothbrush.

"Hey, speaking of kids," he said, holding up the toothbrush toward Mary, "who's the little girl staying with Mom and Dad?"

"Oh, that's Alethea," Mary said casually, "Jess' daughter."

Hearing her name felt like someone threw a bucket of ice-water in his face.

"As in, Jess Serdahl?"

"Yep!"

Pete was dumbfounded. Stung, even, by this revelation, though he knew he had no right to be. He had moved on, why shouldn't she?

"Oh. I didn't know she..." Pete wasn't sure what he wanted to ask. Or what he wanted to hear answers to. "So... who's Alethea's father?"

"We don't know," Mary started, with a hint of adventure in her voice, "Jess has never talked about it. And, you know what else? She's never been in a relationship, either."

"Really?!"

"Really. Not since you two broke up. In fact, I always assumed *you* were Alethea's father." Mary turned and started out the bathroom door.

Pete was stunned. How did she know about his relationship with Jess? They had kept it a secret. Well, he had, at least.

"You thought *I* was... her father? You knew about Jess and me?"

Mary was smirking slyly. "Of course I knew about you two. She told me everything. You might have kept it secret from everybody else, but I knew." She started chuckling. Impersonating a mad scientist. "Muahaha... Oh, I knew."

"Wow. But still, that was years ago. There's no way I can be Alethea's father! She never... she didn't... she wasn't pregnant when I left town. I would've known."

"When was the last time you two did it?" Mary asked, smiling ear to ear.

"I don't know, Mary," he said, "I don't really want to talk about it, to be honest. It was years ago, and I've moved on."

"You left for L.A. what... six years ago, right?"

"Yeah, almost."

"Well..." Mary paused for dramatic effect. "Alethea just turned five in October. You do the math."

He started to feel dizzy. He hadn't even been home for a whole day, and he was already being forced to re-live his painful memories. This is why he hadn't come back over the last six years. He needed the distance to move on. Being in Utica meant being around all the places that belonged to his

135

past self. To his life with Jess, which had left him brokenhearted.

"I don't know what to tell you, Pete. It looks like we *both* might be parents. Ready or not, I guess."

"Huh," is all he managed to say, his mind turning to mush.

"You should go talk to Jess. She's in the hospital - breast cancer. I'm sure it would mean a lot to her if you stopped by. Plus, you can get answers about Alethea."

Mary walked down the hall, leaving Pete alone. He slunk to the floor, kicking the bathroom door closed, and ran his hands through his hair. He was getting a headache thinking about his situation. There were no good options. He could ignore the previous conversation, pretending it never happened, but then he'd have to live with the possibility that he had a daughter. And live with the fact that he had chosen to not know - to abandon her - out of fear.

Of course, finding out if he was the father was scary, too. Seeing Jessica again. Having old feelings resurface. And, what if he found out that someone else was Alethea's dad? That meant Jess had rebounded with some other guy right after he left. That her rejection was worse than he knew. But then again, if he was the father, what would that say about him as a person? That Jess thought her child would be better off without him? And what would happen, exactly? What would he want to happen? Would he want to become a part of Alethea's life after being absent for the first five years? And how would Eyana feel about this possible plot-twist?

Everywhere he looked, Pete saw opportunities for his life to be upended. Maybe even ruined. He wanted to crawl into a hole somewhere and hide away. But at the same time, a new, unfamiliar feeling was beginning to emerge. Maybe it was spurred on by seeing Mary's vulnerability. Maybe it was the first fragment of fatherly instincts. Whatever the case, Pete realized what mattered most to him in this moment was Alethea. He wanted her to be taken care of. To know her father, if that's what he was. And, for the first time in a long time, he was ready to risk his own pain for someone else.

Forty-five minutes later, he was in the oncology wing at St. Luke's, listening to Jessica Serdahl talk about their breakup six years ago. She talked about how she had loved him, but knew she had to let him go. About the surprise pregnancy and the difficult choice to sacrifice herself. To keep her secrets. To absorb all the shame and humiliation so he could be free. So his family reputation could remain untarnished. About how Alethea had made it all worthwhile. How every time she looked at their daughter, she saw Pete's eyes. About how she always knew that someday he'd re-enter the picture. That when they needed him, he would find his way back to Utica. About the doctors discovering cancer two months earlier. About her praying for the chance to tell him about Alethea. About how she had dreamed, two nights ago, that he would be coming into her hospital room exactly like this.

December 24th, 4:07PM (30 Minutes Before)

Tim, Jr. (Timmy)

Timmy slipped through the saloon doors, entering the dining room, his stomach in knots. He hadn't planned on making the announcement this soon, but the last few hours had convinced him. He had realized that he'd never have the courage to consciously choose this. He'd never be brave enough to tell his dad the truth. So, focusing on this unsurmountable nightmare was making him physically ill. His anxiety was inching closer to a panic attack with every passing hour. He just wanted it to be over with.

Then, there was the grocery store disaster this morning. As his mom had gone on a tirade during the car ride home, he was reminded that he couldn't wait for his parents to change, either. Dad wouldn't be ready for this if he were on his deathbed. Whatever the consequences may be, he had to rip the band-aid off. He was going to come out to his family today. He chose the chair closest to the stairs, which also happened to be nearest to the front door. Two escape routes he might need in a few minutes.

Linda placed the mashed potatoes on the table, next to the beans. The final touch to her culinary masterpiece. The herbs from the roasted chicken blanketed the room with a familiar odor, which normally would lead to mouth-watering and stomach-grumbling, but Tim had no appetite this time. After his father said grace, Tim filled his plate as he usually would have, keeping his head down to avoid eye-contact with Linda. His plan was to wait for her to have her mouth full - so she

138

was unable to derail him - and then say his piece quickly and loudly, before leaving the room. Thankfully, Linda had already fed Alethea and set her up with a movie upstairs. She wouldn't have to witness the resulting display of bigotry and vitriol. Now all he needed was a break in the conversation. His mom took a bite. Timmy took a breath and cleared his throat. Then, his dad asked about tonight's Christmas Eve service.

Tim, Sr.

Over the last twenty-four hours, a knot had formed in Tim's stomach. Everyone and everything was against him. Eyana had spent the night with Pete, even though everyone knew where he stood on that issue. Linda had been overly sensitive and a bit feisty - even more than usual for this time of year. And then there was Pete's announcement last night. They had made it through most of the seventy-minute drive home from the Syracuse airport without any incident. But then, as they pulled into the driveway, Pete informed him that he would be staying home instead of joining the family for the Christmas Eve church service. It was hard enough to know that his son, and former associate pastor, was no longer going to church each week, and drifting away from the faith. But for him to make such a public statement by staying home on Christmas Eve?! This was a new level of disrespect.

Christmas Eve was special. It was the one service where every family that ever visited the church would come marching in the doors, talking with him afterward and reading the bulletin, acting like they were regulars. He saw this sermon as a sort of tryout. If he did well enough, perhaps a few of those families would come more often and the church wouldn't be in such a precarious position. And maybe, if his kids were all there together, it could resuscitate their faith and rejuvenate the family.

Tim looked up at the four family members and two guests sitting around the table. Six strangers, it felt like. He decided to bring up the service. It was one thing for Pete to make a stand privately, with a last-second comment in the driveway to just him. But here, he would have to face Linda and the whole family.

"So, about tonight," he started, acting as if it were a foregone conclusion that everyone would attend, "please make sure to be at the church early. By six-thirty at the latest."

"Dad," Pete tried to interject, but Tim kept rolling.

"And I'd imagine your mother would like it if everyone sat together in the usual spot. Right, Linda?"

Linda gave Tim a look of warning as she answered. "I think what your father is trying to say, is that *if* you are coming to the service tonight, you're welcome to come whenever you'd like and sit wherever you'd like. I'll be in my usual seat and of course, everyone is welcome to sit with me, if they want to."

His stomach knot tightened a little. Tim wasn't used to his wife being this direct. This obstinate.

Mary tried to ease the tension by asking about his plans for tonight's sermon. Tim thought this might be a good opportunity to offer some guidance to his children, while honing his sermon in the process. Two birds, one stone.

"Well, Mary," he began, "I'll be preaching from the Christmas story. I'm focusing on the Virgin Birth, using Jesus' mother Mary as an example of the sort of purity that should mark our lives, too."

Pete cocked his head back and raised one eyebrow - a look he learned from his dad. "Wait, let me get this straight. You're going to talk about sexual purity on Christmas Eve?"

"Not exactly how I'd--" Pete cut him off.

"You get one chance to talk to all those once-a-year-members, and everyone's family that's in town, and it being Christmas and all... but the one topic you think is best to discuss is not having sex outside of marriage?"

Tim felt white-hot. He knew Pete was just trying to get a rise out of him, but it was working. His son had crossed the line.

"Listen, Peter," he said firmly, "has it ever occurred to you that this might be an important issue? Our church has seen its fair share of immorality, and in today's culture, purity is under attack from every angle. Mary's example is highlighted in the Christmas story multiple times, so I'm going to include it in my sermon. Whoever is in the audience isn't my concern, I'm just telling the truth!" He could tell Pete was backing off, but Tim couldn't help it. He had to put the final nail in the coffin. "And another thing - I don't appreciate your tone. Obviously, this topic gets under your skin. Maybe that's why you're trying to get out of coming tonight! I wonder what might be the problem for you, Pete?! Is it that you're feeling guilty about shacking up with your girlfriend?!"

His son wasn't backing off anymore. Tim watched as Pete let his fork fall to his plate and tried to swallow his mouth-

141

full of chicken, preparing his defense. Linda gasped her disapproval. Tim wondered if he'd gone too far. He tried to think of something to say that might soften the blow - something to prevent an all-out screaming match - but before he could say anything further, Mary interrupted.

Mary

Normally, she'd stay out of these conversations. It was better to just let Pete and Dad have it out. But this time, listening to her dad go on and on about premarital sex and those promiscuous women having children outside of marriage, Mary lost control. She whipped her napkin onto her plate and scooted her chair back from the table, the wooden feet scraping across the linoleum. She was planning to just walk out on the conversation. Send a somewhat-subliminal message. But whichever part of her was pulling the strings had a different idea. Before she realized what was happening, Mary was shouting at her dad.

"Why are you so obsessed with the virginity of all these women!? It's like some sick fantasy or something, Dad!"

Everyone froze, watching the patriarch of the family. Her dad was completely caught off guard. His face was flushed, and he was staring at Mary in surprise, wincing as if her words had physically hurt him. Mary wasn't done.

"Why do you care so much about who's having sex?! And if someone has a baby outside of marriage… why is that so terrible to you?" She was shouting now, tears welling up. "Why is that so bad!?"

The hormones from her pregnancy were colliding with the emotions from finding out about it this morning, yet her mind was clear. She knew what needed to be said, and was delivering the information with the kind of passion and feeling that only a pregnant mother had access to. Normally, she was the one person who never showed emotion, who was always in control, but something had snapped. She was now stripping herself bare and making herself vulnerable. Maybe this child was changing her sooner than she expected.

While Mary was still petrified about becoming a mother, this morning's talk with Pete had helped her embrace the idea. She was even starting to want to be a mom, for the first time in her life, but she was so unsure of everything that came along with being a *single* parent. This baby was going to drastically change her whole life. She would be trading in her freedom and adventurous spirit for responsibility and commitment. And how would people react to this news. How would they treat her and her little one? Would she be able to protect them from the judgment and mistreatment? Could she provide for them? She wanted to know that they'd be ok. Then, she recalled the stories about the scarlet cords.

There were a few Bible stories Mary learned as a kid that were about important women. Of course, back in those days, a woman's importance was measured by the male children she gave birth to, but the stories still stuck out in her memory. The first story was about a widow named Tamar, who eventually became a prostitute to survive, seduced a man named Judah, and got pregnant. When she started showing, the whole town got really angry about the unwed pregnancy. So mad, in fact, that they were ready to kill her, but Judah convinced them to spare her life in exchange for her silence about his involvement. Her life for his reputation. She ended up having twins, and the midwife wrapped the scarlet cord around the first baby's hand, to mark it as the oldest. And you'd think that those twins were destined to obscurity, marked by society as sub-human bastards. But even though they were the result of prostitution and born out of wedlock, they ended up becoming the patriarchs for two of the twelve Tribes of Israel.

The other story was also about a prostitute - Rahab. She saved the lives of some Jewish spies, shared some special prophetic knowledge she'd received from God, and was spared when her city, Jericho, was destroyed. The scarlet cord was her lifeline - hung out the window so the troops would know who to rescue.

Later on, she had a child, and we eventually find out that her kid, Boaz, was King David's great-grandpa, which was a big deal in Bible times! It didn't matter how many Bible verses Mary had forgotten over the years, these stories had stayed with her.

Mary made a mental note to herself - she was going to craft a scarlet necklace. Something to remind her every day throughout this pregnancy that she would be ok. That God still loved her. And her baby. Then she remembered another child born to a single mom.

"Dad! Think about what the Christmas story is all about… and what you're even going to preach about tonight. I mean, the Virgin Mary had baby Jesus before she was married! She was a single mom!"

Mary saw her mom trying to say something. Attempting to shut this conversation down, but she wasn't stopping.

"I just wish you would move on. Start caring about something else! There are so many real problems in the world to worry about, but you can't get past women having premarital sex. You just sit there and pass judgment on people like me. But think about Rahab. Or Tamar. And Mary." The words were coming faster than she could organize them into sentences. She let the tears flow, shouting at the ceiling. "Men are so... it's not fair! And... but... it's going to be ok. I can raise a child! I don't need a husband. I can be on my own. I don't care what any of you think! I'll have a scarlet cord. And my baby might become a tribe. Or a king! I'm going to be just fine."

Her dad finally spoke.

"What... what are you saying, Mary?"

She wiped her eyes, looked across the table into Linda's wide eyes, and whispered, "I'm pregnant."

December 24th, 4:29PM (8 Minutes Before)

Pete

Pete put his arm around his older sister, shielding her from the onslaught of questions. Dad was blowing a gasket. Mom was asking about who the father was. Timmy was staring straight ahead in shock. The whole scene was utter chaos, and Pete was embarrassed of his family. Angry. Defensive of Mary.

This was not how an announcement of pregnancy was supposed to go. Getting lambasted by your father and quizzed by your mother?! He thought about how fragile Mary was when they talked about everything this morning. And how she had always taken care of him, even keeping secrets for him all these years. And about how good it felt to take care of her in return. Then he thought back on his morning trip to St. Luke's and his talk with Jess Serdahl. And explaining everything to Eyana, afterward. Then he was reminded of the pillar of fire.

There was this story. One his parents used to tell him from the Old Testament, where God put a cloud all around the Jewish people escaping Egypt. A cloud during the day that turned into a pillar of fire at night. It protected them. And when Pharaoh sent his chariots after them, the cloud stood in the way, blocking the Egyptian army so the Israelites could escape. Pete smiled, knowing what he needed to do. He was going to become Mary's cloud.

Standing out of his chair, he clinked a butter knife off his glass, raising it in the air as if to give a toast.

"Well, well, well. First of all, my congratulations to Mary!" He said loudly, demanding the spotlight. "I couldn't be happier for you. And for myself, too, because I'll be an uncle - assuming you decide to keep it."

Pete was gambling with the last bit. He knew that was sure to get a reaction, and it did. His dad started yelling again, but this time it was at *him* instead of Mary. The cloud was starting to work.

"Ok, ok. Calm down! Listen! I too have an announcement to make." He waited a few seconds for everyone to settle. "I found out today… that I'm a father! Well, actually, that I've been a father for over five years."

"What?" Linda gasped, "what does that mean?"

"It means, Mom, that Alethea is my daughter."

His mom looked incredulous. Eyana put her hand in the small of his back, rubbing back and forth. His dad went pale, looking confused. Looking hurt. Betrayed.

"What are you saying, Peter!? Are you saying that this whole time… it was *you?!? You're* the father?"

Pete sat down and crossed his arms, pleased with himself, watching his dad implode.

"Th-that's impossible! That means… that means you two were sleeping around while, what? While you were a pastor on my staff? Do you realize what you've done?! You've tarnished the family name! You've destroyed everything that we've worked to build. How could you do this to me? To your family?!"

His dad was huffing and puffing. He couldn't compute everything that was happening.

"First, Mary's pregnant," his dad shouted, "and now, you basically tell us that you were living in sin behind my back for years! What's next?! Timmy... do *you* have any sexual immorality you'd like to share??"

Tim, Jr. (Timmy)

Timmy was trying to make sense of what was happening. Of what he was feeling. On the one hand, he felt upstaged. He had finally found the courage to make his announcement. He was ready to face his family, but before he had the chance to disappoint his father, Mary and Pete had beat him to it. And yet, on the other hand, his siblings may have made Timmy's situation easier. Maybe, if he were to just add his announcement on top of this train wreck, his dad's reaction would be split between the three of them. He'd no longer be in the crosshairs. And besides, his father did just ask... No one could blame him for answering the question.

He felt like King David from the Sunday-School stories. Young David actually, from before he became a king. Ready to come out of the shadows. Out of the closet. David was the youngest sibling just like Timmy, and the Bible even specifically called him "handsome, with beautiful eyes." Phillip describes Timmy the same way. And David also had to find a way past the limitations of his father - who was always overlooking him and preferring his older siblings. Demanding that he stay home and remain a simple shepherd. It took Timmy three years after high school to find a way out of Utica and into the Big Apple. And there's more - although people didn't really identify with sexual orientations in biblical times, Tim, Jr., was pretty sure King David and his best friend Jonathan were more than just roommates. There was one verse Timmy had read over and over when he was in high school, where David tells Jonathan that his love is better than the love of a woman. Whether he was bisexual or gay, or even queer, King David was the hero Timmy needed. David helped him feel safe. Seen by someone. God, maybe. And so, just like his Old Testament hero, Timmy needed to confront his fears, slay his Goliath, and declare his love for Phillip publicly.

"Actually, Dad, I have something to say, too," he said, standing up and grabbing Phillip's hand for support.

"Timmy, don't," Linda said, placing her hand on the table.

He looked her in the eyes with what he hoped was a reassuring and gentle expression.

"It's ok, Mom. It's better to have everything out in the open."

Linda's eyes were darting back and forth between her husband and Timmy. A ball of nervous energy, unsure what to do. His dad was looking in Timmy's general direction, but something didn't seem right. His eyes weren't focused. Like a boxer between rounds.

"Dad, I need you to know the truth. You need to know who I am and... ...and how I feel about Phillip."

Linda stood up, leaning in toward the center of the table a little, partially blocking Timmy's view of his dad. "Timmy, stop! Don't do this!"

And then, as confidently as he could, he belted it out. "Dad... I'm gay! And Phillip and I are getting married!"

149

Pete smiled his approval at his brother. Mary clapped her hands twice in front of her mouth. Phillip stood up, joining his future husband. Timmy stared at his dad, waiting for his reaction, but he didn't respond. Instead, Linda slammed her hand on the table, rattling all the dishes and causing Timmy to flinch.

Then she cried out, "I HAD AN ABORTION!"

Linda

Linda's heartbeat thundered in her ears. Her ribcage was vibrating. Head spinning. Everything was falling apart, and it was all her fault. She knew the reason Tim was so worried about pre-marital sex, arguing with Pete and Mary. Why he was so hung up about Jessica Serdahl. Linda's original sin had unleashed a curse on her family, pulling everyone into its vortex. A dark cloud had been hovering over this family, all because of what happened in 1978.

They had been dating for two years. Tim was the young up-and-coming preacher on staff at a large church in Albany and she was the church secretary. They were the talk of the congregation. The young God-fearing couple representing the future. And as their relationship went on, they found themselves getting more and more physical. On New Year's Eve, 1977, they lost their virginities in Tim's studio apartment. Tim felt pleasure. Linda felt loved. And so, over the next few weeks, they had sex eighteen times.

She knew how guilty Tim felt about it all. He tried over and over to stop, but Linda kept finding ways to get them alone. Of course, they both felt the guilt of breaking God's rules and secretly carrying on this sinful relationship, but Linda mostly blamed herself. She had seduced a man of God. Dragged him into a sinful life of impurity.

Then, in early February, Linda missed her period. She waited a week before secretly going to the doctor to get confirmation, but she already knew she was pregnant. The nurse gave her a hug and told her how lovely it was. She could give the good news to her husband on Valentine's Day! Linda wept in the parking lot.

While she was overjoyed about the possibility of being a mother, she knew that this was the one thing that simply could not happen. Tim had made that abundantly clear. This was the only thing that could derail his career. It would destine the two of them for a life of being ostracized. Living as outcasts from the church. So, Linda kept her pregnancy a secret, even from Tim.

For days, she didn't sleep. She couldn't eat. She agonized over what to do. She could run away and raise the child on her own somewhere, leaving Tim's reputation intact. Or maybe they could get married! They had already begun discussing marriage and she knew that he was going to propose soon. But they'd have to get married within the month to keep her secret. Tim wouldn't go for that, and people would be suspicious, anyway. There was only one viable choice.

On February 23, 1978, Linda got an abortion before anyone knew anything. It destroyed her. The secrets. The guilt. The anger over giving up her own baby. Over it being her burden to carry, and hers alone. She made sure that they didn't have sex again until their wedding night - New Year's Eve, 1978. As the organ played and Linda walked the isle - the pastor's wife, pure and perfect, on display for all to see - she silently made a promise to herself. A second vow to be solemnly sworn during this holy ceremony. She would never prioritize anyone or anything above her own child again, should God allow her to have any.

For forty years, she had upheld that promise, with very little difficulty. But today, witnessing Mary and Pete confessing at Christmas dinner, Linda's resolve was being challenged. Her choices from long ago were reverberating today, and she wasn't going to sit by, letting her children take the beating for it. She wasn't going to be like Sarah.

There's a story in Genesis, that Tim liked to bring up in sermons, about Abraham being asked by God to sacrifice his son, Isaac. Abraham and Sarah had gone through so much to even have a child, and now that they finally had one in their old age, God was testing Abraham's faith, so they say, by asking him to perform child sacrifice. Linda hated that story. Why was every father she'd ever known so willing to sacrifice their kids? And what kind of god demands child sacrifice as a test of loyalty?! And what sort of mother, Linda often wondered, would stand by and allow her baby to be killed in the service of that deity?

In the story, Abraham doesn't have to go through with it. God decides to murder an innocent, injured animal to appease his need for sacrifice, instead. But it didn't work out that way for Linda. She had submitted, like Sarah. She had marched herself into the clinic and laid her baby down on the altar, sacrificing her only child so that God's chosen messenger could continue to serve. But never again.

Timmy was standing up. She had to act fast, before he too was in harm's way. She stood and filled the space between her husband and her youngest child, laying herself on the altar, tying the ropes tight, sacrificing herself to save him. There was no telling how Tim would react. She paused for the briefest of moments, wondering if this would end their marriage. Wondering if she even cared. Hoping Timmy hadn't yet said too much. Then she sprang into action.

Linda slammed her hand down on the table and passionately confessed. She explained everything. The secrets. The pregnancy. The abortion.

Tim collapsed, falling out of his chair to the floor.

December 24th, 4:35PM (2 Minutes Before)

Tim, Sr.

Tim couldn't catch his breath. The flurry of sentences from everyone around the table were landing like a boxer's punches. Jab, jab uppercut. Left hook. Haymaker. He felt each blow physically. His ribs were being crushed. His left arm tingled. His chest burned.

He was on autopilot with the conversation, delivering the same rehearsed speeches about godliness and family loyalty, while his mind tried to sort through it all.

Mary's right, you know. You are obsessed with this topic. She probably knows why, too. They all see right through you.

He tried to focus on breathing. Inhale. Exhale.

You're a hypocrite! Running around policing everyone else's sex lives to appease your own guilt. Your kids have abandoned you; your wife is barely hanging on… all because of you and your self-righteousness.

Mary made her announcement. It felt like a clamp was closing around his torso, snapping a few ribs. He was transported back to when he and Linda were dating. He had just started out as an associate pastor. She was a bright, respected leader and everyone knew she was going places. She was out of his league, and it was obvious. The longer they were together, the more he pushed her toward intimacy. He was so insecure, and he needed something to keep her connected to him. Tethered to him. For weeks, leading up to New Year's Eve, 1977, he brought them closer and closer to the edge, until finally, he convinced her to go all the way right after the ball dropped.

For the next several weeks, Tim tried to get Linda in bed every chance he got. And afterward, he would find subtle ways to suggest that she was the one responsible for their sinful behavior. That this was her fault; he was innocent. A collection of micro-messages - little comments in his prayers or points in his sermons - all communicating one theme: he was an upright man of God, and she was a temptress, seducing him. And, at the same time, he kept reinforcing how devastating it would be for her if anyone found out about their misdeeds. She'd be dishonored. Marked with a scarlet 'A'.

Tim knew it was wrong. Sick and twisted, really. But there were forces more powerful than guilt. He had been desperate to not lose her. But now, forty years into marriage, he finally saw it all for what it was. Who he had been. What he had done. How his multi-decade smear campaign had backfired. How he'd forcefully secured her loyalty from the very beginning, without ever gaining her love.

The tingling in his arm turned to sharp, shooting pain. Like a gun firing bullets from his shoulder, down and out his index finger.

Pete shared his news. The room started to spin. While one part of him mindlessly argued with his son, his thoughts traveled back to Valentine's Day, 1978. He and Linda were at dinner, and she was asking about babies and wedding dates. Wondering what he'd do if she got pregnant. Tim did not react well. He was a pastor. They couldn't get pregnant. This was exactly the sort of conversation he didn't think they needed to have. She should know her place. And if they did get pregnant, that would be her fault, too. She would have to keep him out of it and deal with the consequences silently. There would be no emergency wedding. No stepping down from his career and admitting their impropriety.

Tim had stormed out of the restaurant, leaving Linda to pay the bill. As they drove away, he apologized for his temper. Linda nodded her forgiveness, submissively. But then, as he dropped her off at her home, Linda made it clear that the fallout from an accidental pregnancy would be too devastating. Too destructive for them to risk it by continuing to sleep together. They would have a sexless relationship from that day forward. Tim went ring shopping the next day.

As Timmy stood up at the other end of the table, Tim's vision went blurry. Everything seemed in slow motion. But, while his body was being torn apart, his mind was finding the last bits of needed clarity. His whole adult life, Tim realized, he had been sacrificing everything and everyone on the altar of his reputation. It may have started with Linda, but it continued with the church and each of his kids. If anyone made choices in their life that compromised Tim's standing or authority as a pastor, they were cast off. When someone acted contradictory to his teachings, he took it personally.

His whole public life had been one long sermon. He had, as far as anyone else could tell, stayed faithful to God, and everyone else should take care to do the same. If not, they suffered the consequences. It was obvious to him now why he had kept up this facade of piety for decades. Why he had obsessively and meticulously orchestrated his reputation as a pure and holy man of God. He was trying to outrun his past. Trying to make up for breaking the rules with Linda. To prove his worth to God. To himself.

Linda was standing up now, too. The sensation in Tim's chest localized just to the left of center, as if someone had stabbed him with a knife. He'd never felt such intense pain before. He tried to scream. His eyebrows shot upwards, but there was no sound. He couldn't get enough air into his lungs to even whisper a call for help. A tidal wave of panic washed over him. He was sure his family was about to witness his death.

Linda threw the knockout punch.

He started falling to the left, out of his chair, helpless to stop it. His whole body had shut down. It felt like his sternum had exploded and the shock wave was disabling every muscle in its path. Laying on the cold floor, he couldn't move. There were voices yelling, but they sounded miles away. Too muffled to understand the words. He saw shadows moving. Pairs of feet scurrying to his aid, perhaps.

As he surrendered to the storm of pain and chaos, Tim said a silent prayer, promising to change his ways if he were to survive. It was long past time to stop running from the truth of who he was. Each of his children had held up a mirror at the table. He'd seen his own broken and flawed humanity reflected in each of them and realized how incapable of judging them he was. Tim was ready to give up his gavel. To be a father instead if it wasn't too late.

He also promised to take responsibility for what he had done to Linda. His abusive behavior had led to even more destructive consequences than he had imagined. He could hear the decades of pain and grief in her confession, and he knew he was responsible for all of it. He begged God to give him one more chance to talk to Linda. He needed to ask for forgiveness.

Then, ever so slowly, the room faded away and everything went dark.

December 24th, 8:21PM (4 Hours After)

The emergency room waiting area at St. Luke's was eerily empty, except for the Jones family. Pete and Eyana read to Alethea. Across from them, Timmy laid his head on Phillip's shoulder and closed his eyes. Mary and Linda held hands. Each family member silently re-examined Christmas dinner in their memories, searching for evidence that the heart attack was their fault.

Over the next seven minutes, a doctor shared the details of Tim's "coronary event", the procedures she'd used to treat it, and all the necessary steps to recovery. The EKG ran during the ambulance ride had confirmed what was happening, and they had put Tim on blood thinners as soon as he had arrived at the emergency center. During the two and a half hours that followed, Doctor Langford and her team found two blockage-points in arteries near the heart, thanks to the angiogram she ran, and performed a coronary angioplasty at both sites to restore blood flow. She also told the family that, as a part of the operation, she inserted stents in both locations, which are permanent and will help prevent future buildup or blockage. Tim would need to stay in the hospital for a few nights, but ultimately, he'd be ok. Stress was named as the culprit. Rest was the antidote. Along with regular doctor visits, a change in diet, and a few tweaks to his lifestyle.

Tim, Sr.

It took Tim a few minutes after waking up to recognize where he was. It was obviously a hospital room, but he wasn't sure what had happened. Why he was there. He took a mental rollcall over his body, hoping to find something that would make sense of his situation. No broken limbs. No sharp pain or muscles that wouldn't move. He mostly just felt weak and tired. And very sore in his torso. He had complained about feeling like he'd been hit by a truck hundreds of times, but this time was different. Those were plastic toy trucks, and this was an eighteen-wheeler.

A nurse came by to check on the two IV bags dripping liquids through tubes into his arm and began to talk through his recovery process. When she said the words "heart attack", all the events of the last twenty-four hours came rushing back. He remembered everything in an instant - the stress at church, the family dinner a few hours earlier, the clarity about his life - how he'd pressured and judged his children, pushing them away, and his relationship with Linda. The secrets. The manipulation. The dominant abuse of power. His chest tightened and he felt bile rising in his throat.

Although the recovery process, as the nurse was explaining it, was going to be difficult, Tim wasn't worried about that. Instead, he was re-experiencing his "Road to Damascus" moment during dinner. The clarity. The regret. The surrender. Tim desperately wanted to change. To be better. He was determined to be, he just wasn't sure how. He couldn't imagine what it would be like to move past his judgments about what was right and wrong. He didn't know how to relate to people without the superiority that came along with having their respect. Always being the authority.

Along with his fears and concerns about trying to change, he also wondered about the church. Even though he and Linda had been married before moving to Utica, it still felt like he needed to come clean to the elders about everything in his past. Like his whole ministry as a pastor had been built on lies. Plus, there were new revelations that would come out as well. His daughter is pregnant. His son is gay. How would all of this be received by his congregation. Will he be out of a job soon? But the church could come later. Tim needed to talk to his family first. He had to promise Mary he'd be there for her. He had to apologize to Pete. To hug Timmy. And most of all, he needed to take responsibility with Linda. To ask her forgiveness.

Over the next twenty-four hours, Tim's body took its first baby steps in a marathon of healing. The family did the same, as each one took their turn spending time at his bedside in between nurse-ordered naps. Linda went first. She shared the details of 1978, the vow she made to herself on their wedding day, and her longing for the family to be at peace. Tim listened. He asked for forgiveness. Forgiveness for gaslighting her. Forgiveness for punishing Linda instead of taking responsibility for his own actions. For pushing their children away instead of holding them tight.

Mary asked for support as she progressed toward motherhood. Her child wouldn't have a father, so they would really need their grandfather. Tim assured her that he'd be there for her and for her baby, even though he'd still be worried about her trying to raise a child without a partner.

Pete shared the story of how he demanded too much of Jessica Serdahl. How that led to his heart being broken - the real reason he ran to L.A. Tim confided in his son about his own similar failures, ancient and recent. He regretted being absent from Pete's life the last six years and asked for a new start.

Timmy talked about how afraid he'd been of his father, and how he hoped they could start to get to know each other. He properly introduced Phillip as his fiancé. Tim Sr said he would attend the wedding. Though he knew it would probably take some time to come to terms with his son's sexuality, he was going to work at it. He'd listen to his son's story. He'd get to know Phillip. He wasn't going to let any sense of self-righteousness get in the way anymore.

Over the next three days, the family shuttled back and forth to St. Luke's, until they brought Tim to the house. Once he was back home on Edgewood Street, when he wasn't resting in his bedroom, he sat in the living room. He wanted to be around his family. To be involved in the conversations.

The Jones family made the best out of the time they had left that week. They played Euchre. They shared childhood stories and picture albums with Eyana and Phillip. Linda made everyone's favorite meals. Except on New Year's Eve. That night, Timmy and Phillip prepared Lasagna to celebrate Tim and Linda's fortieth. Linda said it was better than her own recipe. Pete teased his disagreement.

On their final day together - New Year's Day - everyone shared the plans they had been making for their future. Pete would be moving back to Utica to be near his daughter. Terrified, he had asked Eyana if she would move with him. She said that she'd like to and they agreed to work through it together. Timmy and Phillip set a date for their wedding - June fifteenth, at a cathedral near their apartment in Tribeca. Mary wasn't going to worry about who her child's father was. She knew that they would have all the support they needed.

Linda felt a sense of peace as she took Mary shopping for maternity clothes. Of course, it would be a long and difficult process for this family to reconcile, and she didn't know what the future would hold, or if she could really trust the beginnings of change she saw in her husband. But all the same, she had become grandma to two grandchildren this week. She had gained a future son-in-law and a pseudo daughter-in-law in Eyana. Plus, as the mother of her granddaughter, Jessica was part of the family too. Her heart felt full as she watched Mary in the dressing room mirror. Even if slowly, her family was healing. They were on their way toward being whole.

January 2nd, 5:49PM (9 Days After)

Tim Jones, Jr. (Timmy)

Timmy leaned against Phillip's side, waiting outside the Seattle airport. He should've been exhausted, all things considered, but he was wide awake. Until this past week, he hadn't realized how heavy the burden that he'd been carrying was. Keeping his secrets from his family and the constant fear of being found out - it had all been weighing him down. But now he felt free. Released from a sort of prison. Of course, there was still progress to be made, but the worst was over, and it gave him a spring in his step.

As their Uber approached, he looked over at Phillip and grinned with excitement. They had set a date! He couldn't wait to get to Phillip's childhood home. To see Miriam and Randy. To share the good news with them and start planning the wedding. To tell them about their last week in Utica. Coming out to his family. His dad's heart attack. Everything that happened before it. And after.

They loaded their luggage into the trunk and settled into the backseat. Phillip leaned against the window, ready to fall asleep. Timmy's knee bounced rapidly. It was a forty-five-minute drive to get to the house. Too long to wait. So, on the way, Timmy told their driver the whole story.

THE SVISLACH

We were halfway across the I-90 bridge, when Nathan's blood-curdling scream sent my intestines into my throat.

"OH MY GOD!! WHAT IS THAT?!?!"

My first thought was that some sort of sea creature had arisen from the depths of Lake Washington. I slammed the brakes and frantically looked left and right, searching for something out of the ordinary. Something that would cause a full-grown man to yell like that.

For the first thirty-four minutes, the ride with Nathan had been unmemorable. Mild-mannered and polite, he half-heartedly participated in small talk and commented on the two or three passing sights that were worth a sentence; though, the ride had been mostly unremarkable thus far. The only excitement came from picking him up on the crowded third floor of the airport parking garage, where the rideshare pickups took place.

Airport rides are desirable for drivers, because they are typically long trips and the riders tip well. Dozens of drivers will sit in a holding lot for a few hours, waiting to be matched with a couple returning from vacation or a marketing manager commuting for the week, rather than heading back to the city and looking for fares. And when a few larger flights arrive around the same time, the pick-up zone becomes a nightmarish hurricane of attempted connections.

Nathan, unlike the passengers wandering aimlessly through the driving lanes scanning license plates for a match, was waiting patiently in the shadows when I pulled up. A statue in the midst of chaos, guarding his two rolling bags. Well-worn hiking boots peeked out from under his faded sky-blue jeans. He was wearing a thin red hoodie, with the hood down, exposing his sand-colored buzz cut, and with his five-foot-eight-inch frame, he was someone you wouldn't even notice unless you were looking for him.

We each compared the other with our phone's information and confirmed identities, and then we loaded his bags in the trunk in silence. He had the patience of someone who was inexperienced. Someone who didn't have expectations from doing this every week. As we settled into our seats, I tapped my phone to see where we were headed - the Hilton Garden Inn over on the east side, across Lake Washington. We had forty-five minutes ahead of us.

After a handful of questions, I was able to piece together some basic information. Nathan was starting a new job as a software engineer. He had just flown into town by way of Seoul and was going to start looking for an apartment in the morning. This was his first job out of college, and he was nervous. Nervous about the job. Nervous about moving here. Nervous about living life thousands of miles away from his family. Nervous about living in the United States. As it turned out, this was Nathan's first day in the United States. This was his first day any place other than Belarus.

The rolling grassy hills and the pine wood tree-lined streets of Minsk were the playgrounds of Nathan's youth, and he explored every meter of it. He kept to himself for the most part, preferring the companionship of the rustling wind and pattering rain drops to the fickle friendships of schoolmates. There were two things that never wavered - nature and family. Anytime Nathan felt out of place or a little unsettled, he recentered by solving a puzzle with his mother or taking a stroll outside. Often, he walked along the bank of the Svislach River, which snaked its way down from the northwest, through the city, and out into the countryside. The Svislach was his favorite body of water. It was his favorite anything, really.

It all started on his eighth birthday, when Nathan received a map of Europe from his grandfather, Daniil, that covered the whole kitchen table like a tablecloth when he unfolded it all the way. He loved his map more than any toy or gift he'd received, and he would spend entire afternoons studying every square kilometer of terrain, every twist and turn in the rivers. Thousands of times, his right index finger had traced the Svislach's winding path from the Vileyka Reservoir northwest of Minsk, back and forth through the city and surrounding towns. It would turn west at times, or north in some areas, yet it always found its way back to the southeast and its destined connection with the Berezina, where the Svislach takes on a new identity and continues on its trek.

The water that once streamed past Nathan's gaze as the Svislach, would then gain momentum with each subtle drop in elevation as the Berezina, flowing through Babruysk and then Svietlahorsk, before being reborn as the Dnieper River, about fifty kilometers northwest of Gomel. Continuing with the power of three rivers, this water turned south, running through Loyew, slipping into Ukraine, and then widening out to about five kilometers wide, just north of Kiev. And here, in Kiev, it became a proper waterway. That same water might now be carrying barges or small cargo ships. It might be sloshing against concrete supports for train bridges or being flung by the paddle wheel of a riverboat.

It took two fingers, after Kiev, for Nathan to trace his favorite body of water through Dnipro and Zaporizhzhia, and into its final transformation in the Black Sea. It fascinated him to think about how the water could have multiple lives. The Vileyka, the Svislach, the Berezina, the Dnieper, the Black Sea. And who knows where the water came from before the reservoir - maybe it was originally from the Black Sea and had evaporated into the clouds. Maybe this was all a long journey home.

In the end, each water droplet that reached the Black Sea traveled more than seventeen kilometers from where Nathan lived. And once it arrived, he liked to imagine, it needed to rest up for what came next. Because that was only the first leg of the journey. Once you've made it to the Black Sea, you're only a quick trip through the Bosporus Straight into the Sea of Marmara, and then through the Straight of the Dardanelles to reach the Mediterranean - and you can get anywhere from the Mediterranean!

Nathan watched hundreds of would-be journeyers embarking on this trek from Minsk. Most days it was a leaf or a stick, but other times he would fashion a galley or sloop out of cardboard, wood, and tape. And with every new ship he sent on its way, he would imagine himself at the helm, Grandpa's map in his pocket, waving to onlookers in Kiev, docking for supplies in Istanbul, or maybe even rounding South Africa's Cape of Good Hope. To him, Nathan's beloved Svislach wasn't just a river, it was the gateway to the world.

On Nathan's eleventh birthday, his mother, Karine, brought home a new 1000-piece jigsaw puzzle. When pieced together, it was a river with beautiful trees in full autumn colors flanking each bank. She told him it was the Svislach, but he knew it probably wasn't. Puzzles had already forged the strongest of bonds between Nathan and his mother, but as the two of them put this new puzzle together that afternoon, a weekly tradition was started. Every so often, Karine would add another puzzle to the collection, and every Saturday afternoon they would pull one out and put it together. It was Nathan's favorite part of each week. They only missed two Saturdays that whole year.

Then, twenty days after Nathan's twelfth birthday, Karine was diagnosed with Stage Four Adenocarcinoma - lung cancer. Twenty years of exposure to asbestos at the factory had finally caught up to her. Less than six months later she was dead.

A few hours after his mother's burial, Nathan sat motionless at the kitchen table, staring at the cover flap of his severely worn map. His father, Alexei, was helping Daniil prepare their home for the handful of friends and family coming over. The map's brown ink had faded to yellow, and the seam was ripping in a few places. At twelve, he was old enough to understand the finality of this pain, but not old enough to know how to work through it. He felt helpless and angry and on the edge of breaking down. Tucking the map into his pocket, he walked out the door and spent the rest of the day listening to the comforting sound of the Svislach's rushing water.

Over the next few years, Nathan spent every Saturday morning at the Svislach, and every Saturday afternoon putting together the river puzzle. Alexei and Daniil would clear the table after lunch and find something to busy themselves with elsewhere, while Nathan solved 1000 miniature riddles. No one said a word. No one had to. He missed the calm stability of his mother deeply, and this silent weekly ritual was his way of still feeling connected to her. Of feeling grounded.

Eventually, Nathan permitted his grandfather to sit at the table while he sorted the pieces and placed them in their spots. Daniil took advantage of these opportunities to ask his grandson about his life and listened intently as Nathan described the connection between doing puzzles and learning to code in his Intro to Computer Science class at school.

On Nathan's sixteenth birthday, it was another gift from Daniil that put him on the path to the United States: a laptop. It was the perfect gift for Nathan. With a laptop, he could now take his newfound love - computer programming - and bring it to his first love - the Svislach.

His favorite spot was only a ten-minute walk from his house. There was a bend in the river, just north of Victory Park, where you could sit in the grass, and it felt like you were in a clearing deep in the forest. All the nearby buildings were eclipsed by trees and Nathan could sit in the grass and code until his battery ran low. And when it did, he would shut his laptop and walk alongside the water, all the way to the Drazdy Reservoir, letting the trees blanket him along the way. Within two years, Nathan had learned Python, JavaScript, and C#, and his projects were getting attention from his teachers. In fact, several people were encouraging him to pursue a career in computer science.

Two weeks before his eighteenth birthday, Nathan sat next to his father and grandfather at the table, reading his scholarship offers to them. Alexei laughed with joy as his son tried to explain to Daniil that C# had nothing to do with music and that scripts weren't for acting. Nathan showed them pictures of each university's campus on his laptop as he read the letters, and the three of them would dream about life in those places. Berlin, London, Moscow. But all along, Nathan knew he was going to stay in Minsk. He couldn't possibly leave his home. He couldn't leave his puzzles. He couldn't leave the Svislach. And a new realization was forming inside him as well: Nathan couldn't leave his grandfather. Daniil's health was declining, and he didn't want to miss out on their conversations during his Saturday afternoon puzzle. He had no choice. Alexei had just retired and needed help taking care of Daniil and keeping up with the house, his puzzles and his grandfather were staying here, and no other university had the benefit of being mere steps away from the Svislach.

So, Nathan stayed home and spent his college years doing puzzles with Daniil, going for walks along the river with Alexei, and working on extra side-projects with his favorite professor, Dr. Nemitz. For Nathan, while-loops and scripting were second nature. Algorithms were as easy as lining up the 1000 familiar jut-outs and concave edges to re-create the picture of his pretend Svislach on the puzzle-box lid. Whenever someone would comment on his talents, he would smile and give the credit his late mother's investment in jigsaw puzzles, and when he started receiving job offers from reputable companies, he thought about how he was, in so many ways, the product of his family's support.

Throughout the interview process, everyone kept telling Nathan how beautiful Seattle was. "You'll love how green it is," they'd say. The hiring manager even repositioned her webcam, showing the tree outside her office window to prove her point. It worked. Nathan was swayed by the natural beauty and started to imagine life in the US. But, deep down, he knew he was just dreaming and that he had no intentions of actually leaving home. Daniil was now confined to a hospital bed and Alexei needed Nathan's help more and more with everything. In fact, he had only gone through the application process with a few tech companies to appease Dr. Nemitz. But, by the end of the interviews, after hearing more about nature in the Pacific Northwest than about the job he was interviewing for, a few cracks appeared in his mental armor. He wanted to experience new things in a new place, but he still couldn't imagine living life on his own, so far away from everything he loved. Leaving Minsk would mean that his grandfather would probably die without him there, and then his father would be completely alone. Every positive thought Nathan would have about moving away would get reshaped into feelings of fear or guilt. But eventually, it was a conversation with Alexei and Daniil that convinced him to take the job.

Sitting at the same table where he'd unfolded his map for the first time, and where he'd put together puzzles hundreds of times, Nathan looked down at two birthday gifts. One from his father and one from Grandpa Daniil, who was watching from his bed a few steps away. He opened Alexei's gift first - an iPad. His father explained that he had bought two iPads, one for Nathan and one for himself and had learned how to use Skype so they could keep in touch when Nathan was in the US. It was all Daniil's idea.

"Grandpa knew you needed a friendly nudge," he said.

Nathan felt weak. Overwhelmed by this loving display of strength and support.

As he pulled off the wrapping paper from his grandfather's present, he started to cry. It was a new foldable map, but this time it was a map of the US. Nathan wiped the tear droplets off of the cover, took it over to Daniil's bed, and opened it for them to look at together. His grandfather was beaming with pride, watching his grandson's face as he pointed to where Seattle was.

There were four months between accepting the offer and moving to the US, and Nathan spent every spare minute taking his dad for walks along the Svislach or sitting at Daniil's bedside, convincing himself that everything would be OK once he settled into his new life in the US. His new salary would pay for an in-home caretaker for his grandfather, Alexei would have a weekly reminder to join their Skype call, and Nathan would have lots of nature to keep him company.

Sitting in the back seat of his Uber outside Seattle, looking through the window at the passing pine trees and oncoming traffic, Nathan tried to subdue the lump in his throat. He was unsuccessful. A silent stream of tears rolled down his left cheek. The Svislach finding its way to the Black Sea. He wasn't sure if the tears were from the sadness of leaving Alexei and Daniil back in Minsk, or if he was overcome by the experience of moving to a new country on his own, or if he was so relieved to see so much natural beauty. Everywhere he looked, Nathan saw green. As the Uber driver narrated the sights like a tour guide, Nathan reached into his backpack and ran his finger across the worn edge of his favorite map.

With every kilometer, his heart pumped louder. A mixture of angst and wonder. Everything was foreign and new, yet for some reason it was starting to feel like a homecoming. He was the water that had traveled around bends, through rapids, past shipyards, under bridges, and into the Black Sea, only to find it familiar. He wished he could roll down the window. He wished his arm could reach out and touch the trees whipping past at 110kph.

When the car's tires reached the I-90 bridge, Nathan's eyes took in Lake Washington and his heart raced. He had never seen such dark blue water. He'd never seen the sun shimmer off the surface, like the world's largest disco ball, or the thick green pine trees surrounding the water.

He leaned his forehead against the window glass, feeling like this gorgeous body of water was greeting him. Like an old friend had gone on ahead and prepared a housewarming gift. He imagined some water drops that had comforted him years ago in Minsk, completing their voyage through the Black Sea and the Mediterranean, finding their way into the right rain cloud somewhere above the Pacific Ocean, and then ejecting above this bridge and settling in the lake, waiting for his arrival. Nathan stared at the water, his fingers tingling with excitement and his heartbeat thundering in his ears.

And then he saw it.

Towering over the south end of the lake was something Nathan was completely unprepared for. His mind couldn't make sense of what his eyes were telling him. Like an optical illusion, the earth seemed to touch the sky. Mt. Rainier, a mammoth, majestic, snowy pyramid rising up from the ground, was the first mountain he'd ever seen, and Nathan couldn't contain his joy.

"OH MY GOD!! WHAT IS THAT?!?!"

After a brief skidding stop because the driver thought something was wrong, Nathan spent the final ten minutes of his ride learning everything he could about Mt. Rainier. He had so many questions and he asked all of them. How tall was it? What did it do? How long had it been there? How long would it stay? Can you go there? Can you climb it? What's up at the top?

As the driver answered some questions and laughed at others, Nathan snapped a photo with his phone and saved it to the photo album he'd created for the trip. Once they had crossed over the lake and the mountain was out of view, he pulled the new map Daniil had given him out of his backpack and spread it out over his lap as best he could. He instinctively shifted the map, so he was looking at the Pacific Northwest, and scanned it for Mt. Rainier. It was right where the driver said - southeast of the city. Nathan touched his index finger to the little black triangle symbolizing a mountain, rubbing it softly. Then he closed his eyes, inhaled deeply, and allowed himself to relax for the first time in the thirty-eight hours since leaving Minsk.

Rolling his bags through the hotel lobby and up to the check-in counter, Nathan couldn't stop smiling. He couldn't wait for his first Skype call with Alexei the next day. He was going to share the photo and teach his father all about the mountain.

He checked in, got his key, and headed to his room. After rolling his suitcases into the far corner, Nathan threw open the curtains, carefully unfolded both maps across his bedspread, and then turned and walked out the door. There was only an hour or so until sunset, and he had to go get another look.

THE SKEPTIC

W hen it comes to theories on the unseen mysteries, human beings are squarely split in two. Some of us listen to the ten-minute sales pitch and immediately buy the Essential Oils Starter Kit, while others arrogantly demand to "see the science," considering ourselves modern Einstein's. Some of us know our horoscopes, others meditate or pray, while the non-believers among us shake their heads and roll their eyes.

What about you? Are you a believer or a skeptic? Do you drink the Kool-Aid or label it brainwashing? Where does the burden of proof lie for you? Is it true until disproven, or are you holding out until something can earn your faith with cold hard evidence?

Because the amount of belief or skepticism you have matters. It dictates how you view the world. You might look up at night and see a random smattering of stars strewn across the sky, or you might see Canis Major. Sharing a ride with a stranger could be the moment that your energies intersect with another's, a chance to find your soulmate, or nothing more than two collections of cells inhabiting the same space.

Wednesday, 3:45pm

With my windshield wipers clearing my view every four seconds, I triple-checked the sidewalks and crosswalks for pedestrians, then eased my way onto Broadway – the toughest stretch of road in the whole city. There's enough room in the sequestered bike lanes for a dozen cyclists and it has twenty-foot-wide stroll-ways for sidewalks, but there's nowhere for a driver to pull over and attempt a pickup or drop-off. But still, that problem would only come into play once I located my next passenger, which, thanks to ever-present crowds outside the grunge bars, lingerie boutiques, and consignment shops lining this street, is sort of like "Mission Impossible" (a mission that is entirely possible, given you have adequate technology, a four-person crew, and roughly two hours to pull it off).

My next trip, should I choose to accept it, would begin once I located Heidi near the light-rail station. A needle in a haystack, except the pieces of hay are all wearing dark colored rain jackets and moving briskly in every direction. With my windshield oscillating between blurry and fogged over, I checked my rearview mirror. If I was going to hold up traffic, it would be nice to know who I'd be offending. In today's opposite corner of the ring was a Ford F-250, driven by a blurry ponytailed character, who I hoped was not in a hurry.

Half a block before the light-rail station entrance, I spotted someone sitting on a suitcase. The one still piece in a puzzle of motion. She looked to be in her mid-twenties as far as I could tell, and she was sporting a gray zip-up fleece with black leggings and running shoes. Her suitcase-seat was just a small carry-on, but the mystery traveler had her head between her knees, doubled over. One part of me was hoping that this was Heidi, but another part of me wondered why she was sitting in that position and didn't want her to throw up in my car.

I slowed to a crawl, turned on my hazards, and rolled down the passenger side window. Even if this wasn't Heidi, the least I could do was see if she was alright.

"Excuse me," I shouted, prepping for all possible reactions, "are you Heidi by chance?"

Heidi gave the subtlest of nods as she got to her feet, scooped up her suitcase, and slunk into the backseat.

"I can put that in the trunk if you want," I offered, worrying about how much rainwater was soaking into the cloth seats.

"I'll keep it with me," she said, "I just want to get home."

Heidi had shoulder-length straight black hair, which was made even darker and straighter by the rain. Her face, when not contorted in pain, was gentle and kind, highlighted by a

181

small round nose and the kind of baby blue eyes you normally see in an Alaskan husky. As she half-sat, half-laid in my car, her small frame shaking a little (*from the pain? Or was she cold?*), I felt compassion wash over me.

Blurry Ponytail was now laying on the F-250's horn, so I quickly put the car in drive, fiddling with my phone to see where I was supposed to go next. Heidi let out a slight groan, still holding her stomach.

"Is everything ok?" I asked.

"Yeah," Heidi said weakly, "my stomach's just been hurting since leaving Mexico."

"Mexico!?" That wasn't what I was expecting.

She continued, muttering mostly to herself. "I should've been more careful. I knew I couldn't trust them."

Where was this going? Was she poisoned? Who was "them"? The Mexican drug cartel? Was I going to end up a star witness in court?

"Yes, your honor, before the victim's intestines exploded in my back seat, she mentioned a Mexican gang had poisoned her."

I mean, exciting for sure… but also potentially traumatic. I needed more information if I was going to be useful at all to her attorneys.

"What happened in Mexico?"

"Huh?"

"What do you mean 'you should've been more careful?' Did something happen?"

"No, it's just… you know how you're not supposed to drink the tap water down there? Like, at the resorts and stuff?"

"Sure," I said, trying not to let my disappointment show and also attempting to sound like I knew stuff.

"Yeah, well my friends are idiots and were like, 'whatever, we drink the water all the time. It's fine.' So, I listened to them, like a dumbass, and drank the tap water."

"Oh, I gotcha," I replied.

"Right," she continued, "So now, I'm on the flight back and all of a sudden my stomach starts to hurt, and it gets worse and worse, and now I feel like I'm going to die."

"God, I'm really sorry," I offered, "that really sucks."

"Thanks," she said.

"How long were you there?" I asked, searching for some possible silver lining.

"Just for the weekend, but I guess long enough to get sick. I'm just hoping I don't have a worm or something."

My phone's beeping sound interrupted our conversation, alerting me that we were going to be picking up another passenger. I tried to stop my mind from picturing an earth worm crawling through her intestines and followed the navigation through a couple of turns to the next pickup spot.

Coming to a stop in front of a Thai fusion cafe, I looked around for Amal. The rain had gotten lighter, but water drops had coated all surfaces, so I had to roll down the passenger-side window to see clearly. After a minute, a tall, thin figure emerged from the doorway and approached the car. I guessed that Amal was in his mid-thirties, but his perfectly shaped beard and combover made it hard to tell. He was wearing tight fitting, black jeans that were in the style of motorcycle pants, and a light gray cotton shirt that had the deepest V-neck I'd ever seen. As he got closer, my eyes fixated on the old skeleton key and gold chain hanging around his neck, running perfectly parallel with the V-neck and filling in the gap nicely. *Did he buy that chain specifically for that shirt? The shirt for that chain?*

Amal's cologne entered my car a full three seconds before his body. It was very strong, but pleasant enough. He smelled like the woods, if all of the trees had just showered. Clean. Fresh. A minty woodland.

"Hey everyone," he said cheerfully, as he settled into his seat and buckled his seatbelt. His voice was deep and warm, and made you feel cozy, like the hum of a car engine on a road trip, when you're laying across the back seat. Every word he spoke sounded smooth, like silk. If you were reading this as an audiobook, Amal would be my first choice to give the voiceover.

"You must be Andrew," he said, looking me once over before turning around to look at Heidi. "And you're Heidi?"

He flashed a wide, genuine smile toward Heidi, who smiled back and replied in a chipper voice I didn't know she was capable of, "Yes, that's right - Heidi. Welcome!"

Did she just welcome him…? To what…? My car?

Unsure of where to go from there, I tried to share Heidi's Mexico story with Amal.

"Heidi just got back from Mexico," I said.

"I loooove Mexico," Amal half-sang. "Where did you go? Did you see Chichen Itza? So powerful!"

Heidi started to respond, but Amal continued, barely pausing to take a breath.

"Heidi, tell me about your life. I'm sensing some strong energy in you. Don't leave anything out. What do you love? *Who* do you love? What's your dream? Your passions? Where are you going?"

His machine gun questioning left Heidi stunned for a second, but when she did respond, her voice was strong and pleasant. I wasn't sure if her stomach pain was truly gone or if she was giving an Oscars-worthy performance.

"Well, for starters, I'm going home," Heidi began, "which is more than an apartment - it's my sanctuary."

"Yessss," Amal added supportively.

"I work at a coffee shop, but my true passion is dance." Heidi's voice was getting even stronger. The conversation seemed to be a welcome distraction from the stomachache, which she hadn't shown any signs of since Amal joined us.

They chatted happily for a few minutes, and I focused on the traffic, light rain, and onslaught of pedestrians or cyclists darting in all directions. This part of the city was crowded, rain or shine, and people usually treated the rules of the road as mere suggestions. About thirty feet in front of us, a young techie-looking guy was riding a motorized skateboard on the sidewalk. One of those one-wheeled, futuristic devices of destruction. He was in cargo shorts and a hoodie, sporting the thinnest of backpacks and one of those bike helmets that looks like a hard-shell beanie. The perfect combination of hipster, yuppie, and nerd. He was serpentining through pedestrians, causing a mild panic, and every time he zigged... or zagged left, he was coming within a few inches of hovering right out into the street. One wrong move to dodge a pedestrian or one bump from a crack in the sidewalk and he would become my new windshield decoration. As we came up alongside him, I glided out of the curb lane and into the middle lane. Better safe than the defendant in a vehicular manslaughter case.

I checked my phone's navigation. It wouldn't be long before we got to Heidi's apartment, so I turned my attention back to the hum of conversation between my passengers and prepared to interrupt them.

"Ok, enough about me," Heidi said, "what about you, Amal? Tell me about you."

Amal shifted in his seat so he could watch Heidi's reaction to his next sentence.

"Well… I'm an energy healer."

Heidi paused with her mouth half-open, her lowering eyebrows betraying her suspicion.

"An energy healer," she repeated slowly, "so what does that mean? What do you do?"

Amal smirked with the ease of someone who'd been through many similar interrogations.

"Well, I read people through their energies, and then I use the power of interconnectedness to heal them."

"Heal them from what?" Heidi's skepticism was dripping off every word.

Amal's eyes shifted to the ceiling as he listed off his resume.

"I've healed back pain. I've gotten rid of infections. A lot of chronic pain… like, a lot. And then, there've been those who couldn't orgasm, lifelong depression… just about anything really."

He paused, and for a moment all three of us looked back and forth, making eye contact and connecting without speaking. And even though Amal didn't signal what he was about to do, Heidi and I both knew a demonstration was coming.

Without saying a word, Amal turned even further around so that his shoulders were square with Heidi, and he slowly reached his right hand out in front of him, fingers spread apart. He kept his hand about halfway between his body and Heidi's, moving it up and down and looking intently at her face. Heidi smiled. It was hard not to. A complete skeptic was watching a healer read her energies. This was a showdown.

Amal pulled his hand back and closed his eyes, still smirking.

"Heidi," he called out with his eyes still shut, "I know you don't believe me. I know you think I'm full of shit. But just open yourself up for a moment. I can sense that you need healing."

Amal's eyes remained closed, but Heidi's darted directly to the rear-view mirror to find mine.

The look on her face informed me that Amal had just put the first crack in her skeptical armor.

"Heidi," Amal called out again, "you're in pain, aren't you? You are suffering and I want to heal you."

"Wha... what?" Heidi tried not to give him affirmation, but she also wanted him to continue.

Amal opened his eyes, fixed a calm gaze on Heidi, and took her breath away with his next words.

"Your stomach is hurting you, isn't it!?"

Heidi froze for a second, completely bewildered, and then turned away as her eyes watered. She took about fifteen seconds to gather herself, and then she wiped her face and turned back to Amal, her eyebrows raised high enough that they were disappearing into her bangs.

"How did you do that?" She asked. "How did you do that? How did you do that?" She was a broken record of disbelief.

Amal interrupted her, his work not yet done.

"I take it from your response that I am correct. Which brings us to the big question: Heidi, would you be open to a healing?"

A faint guttural sound escaped Heidi's throat. All of this had caught her by surprise, to say the least.

"No."

There was a pause, and then Heidi continued.

"I mean, I don't know. Can you even do that in here? I don't know. What do you mean? Like, what do you do?"

Amal chuckled and explained how it worked.

"All that has to happen is for you to be open to the healing energy. I would have you lay down and I would try to connect with your energies. If you remain open, your stomach pain will go away."

"Does it hurt?" Heidi asked.

"Ha, no it won't hurt at all, but you might feel a warm sensation or some tingling."

Heidi was looking out the window, weighing the risks. I knew she needed to decide quickly. We were only a minute or two from her apartment. The next streetlight shifted yellow and then red, giving us some extra time.

"I can't believe I'm saying this," Heidi muttered to herself loud enough for us to hear, "Okay, I guess we can try it."

She wedged her suitcase between her seat and mine and laid down with her head behind me and her feet resting on the opposite window. I wondered what the people in the Subaru next to us thought as they watched this whole process. But no matter what it looked like from the outside, the next few moments were some of the most powerful and memorable that have ever occurred inside my car.

Amal leaned halfway out of his seat, placed his left hand behind his seat for support, and reached his right hand out over Heidi's stomach. His fingers were spread as wide as possible and hovering about two inches from her gray jacket. Then, he began whispering very softly, but with intensity. It seemed like it was someone else's voice.

Most of what Amal was saying was too hard to understand, but it didn't matter. The words were more felt than heard. I felt warmth on the surface of my skin. Goosebumps formed on my arms. My body felt weightless. It was as if we were enveloped by this soothing energy and suspended above the street, out of time. Heidi was breathing fast and deep, sighing with every exhale, like a weightlifter pushing through on her final set. I knew that I would never forget this moment, but also that I wouldn't be able to describe it adequately, either.

The high-pitched horn of the Prius behind us brought me back to earth and informed me that the light had turned green. I pushed the accelerator and begrudgingly drove the final few blocks to Heidi's apartment.

Amal's whispers faded and his eyes opened, connecting with Heidi's. Neither spoke while she sat back up and wrestled her suitcase back up onto the seat next to her. I didn't want to be the first to speak, and I wasn't sure what to say. I wanted so badly to ask if the healing worked. Was it the kind of thing that happened instantaneously or would it take twenty minutes to kick-in, like Ibuprofen? It felt a bit awkward to make eye contact, so I just pushed the unlock button and waited.

Nobody moved. Amal and Heidi were still looking at each other, silently. After about twenty seconds, Heidi finally broke the ice.

"That… was… wow."

"Right?" Amal responded.

"Thank you, Amal. That was amazing."

"Thank you for being open."

"I feel so much better. Like… yeah, so much better." She was smiling ear to ear. "I can't believe I let you do that."

Amal smiled warmly and Heidi opened her door.

"Ok," she said slowly, "I'm going to go now. Thanks guys. This was the best ride ever."

She half-skipped her way from the curb to the door, into her building, spinning around to wave. If she still had the slightest bit of stomach pain, she wasn't showing it. I pushed the button on my phone to end Heidi's trip and move on to Amal's destination. He turned to look at me as we pulled back into traffic, giving me a sly look, which I interpreted as saying: "I bet you don't see *that* in your car every day."

Before I share the rest of the story, you must make a choice. I return to my question from earlier: Are you a believer? Was this a genuine healing or a scam? Magic or a cheap trick? As I said, the amount of belief or skepticism you have matters - it dictates how you view the world. How you interpret what you just witnessed. And in this case, how you end the story…

If you're a believer… go to page 193

If you're a skeptic… go to page 197

The Believer's Ending

My eyes kept bouncing back and forth from the traffic to Amal, stunned. I knew something significant had just happened, I just wasn't sure what. Did he really just heal Heidi from stomach pain? And, with what? Connected energies? What does that even mean?

"Amal," I said, trying not to sound like a fan-boy, "That was amazing. I felt the power of that moment too. How did you do that?"

I waited for him to accept my compliment, but he just sat there, smirking.

"I'm sure you probably have this happen all the time. But for me, I mean, that was amazing. How did you do that? Is it exhausting? Do you ever screw it up?"

Amal rolled his eyes gently. "Of course, I screw it up from time to time... just like anything."

"Wait, what?! What do you mean?"

"I mean, you can't always read people that easy, and sometimes you guess wrong."

"Guess?!?" I shouted at him, trying to process what he was saying. "You were guessing? I thought you were reading her energies or something!? Isn't that what you said?"

He chuckled at my naivety. "You bought that, huh?"

"What are you saying, Amal? That was all just a trick or something?!"

"You could call it that," he said. "It's sort of a mix of things. One part psychology, one part observation, and one part magic trick." He paused as if he was trying to come up with the perfect metaphor, before shaking his head and continuing. "Look, I just observe how people are acting, I get them talking so I can read them, and then I make an educated guess. If I act confidently, it usually works."

I was still confused, but my embarrassment was overtaking confusion by the second.

"So, if you're not reading energies, how did you know that Heidi had stomach pain?"

"That was easy," he said, "I saw her holding her midsection and wincing before I even got in the car."

"Wow," I responded, "I feel like a total idiot falling for your con."

We arrived at his destination, and I pulled over to the curb. Amal swung the passenger door open and placed his right foot on the sidewalk, ready to pounce. I thought about how many times a day he must do this to people. I wondered who his next target would be. His calm voice came as a jolt.

"Andrew, just because I make educated guesses, doesn't make it a con. Heidi did really have stomach pain."

"I know she did, but fake energy healings don't help that."

He smiled. "You see everything in black and white, don't you?! When she lays down and takes deep breaths, and she's convinced that her energies can heal her stomach pain... you'd be surprised how many times that's all someone needs. Our bodies are supernatural. With the power of belief, we can heal ourselves from a lot of pain and suffering."

Amal stepped out of the car and leaned down to look at me while I processed everything he'd just said.

"Okay," I said slowly, "so you're saying that you help people... what? Believe?"

"Exactly."

"Believe in what, exactly?"

"Look at it like this - I believe in people, but sometimes they need a little help believing in themselves."

He shut the car door with a flourish and headed off toward the building entrance. I ended his trip on my phone, put the car in gear, and merged into traffic in a daze, unsure of what I had just experienced.

The End (Go to page 201)

The Skeptic's Ending

My eyes kept bouncing back and forth from the traffic to Amal, stunned. I knew something significant had just happened, I just wasn't sure what. Did he really just heal Heidi from stomach pain? And, with what? Connected energies? What does that even mean?

"Amal," I said, putting on the tone of an insider who knew better. He didn't have to pretend anymore. I knew this was all a sham. "That was impressive. You're good."

I waited for him to accept my compliment and to explain his trick, but he just sat there, grinning, patiently waiting for me to continue.

"Okay, how did you do it? Like, for real though."

"What do you mean?" Apparently, he was going to keep up the ruse.

"I mean, how did you do the trick? How did you know her stomach was hurting?"

"Andrew, Andrew, Andrew," he said, scolding me for my disbelief. "That was not a trick. I told you exactly how I did it, I read her energies."

"You mean to tell me that you just held your hand out at a total stranger for ten seconds and boom - you can see their pain? Come on, man."

"No," Amal said, "of course not."

"I knew it."

"No," he continued, "that is not how it works. It takes longer than that."

197

"What do you mean?" I asked. This was not the tell-all I was expecting.

He said, "Sometimes it takes a few minutes and sometimes it takes hours. You just have to practice being present to the energies within others and pay attention. With Heidi, I was trying to read her energy before I even got in your car. I could tell that something was wrong from the sidewalk. Her coloring was too dark."

"What coloring?"

"Her aura. Everything was faded and dark until I got her talking."

"I see."

"Yeah, and then the longer she went, the more I could tell the source of the darker energy was in her midsection."

"Because it was dark?" I asked.

"Um, more like her stomach wasn't emitting light the same as the rest of her. It's a little complicated."

"Right," I said flatly, with a dash of sarcasm.

"You don't believe me," Amal said, "you think I'm just making this up."

"Kind of," I said.

We were getting close to his destination. If I was going to pry his secret out of him, I had to act quickly.

"Why don't you read my energy," I suggested. "If you read me wrong, you have to admit it was just a trick, and if you are successful, then I'll admit you are a witchdoctor or whatever."

He laughed, but intensified his stare at me and said, "Ok, then."

He looked me in the eyes and then moved his body away from me, up against his door, taking me in.

"Don't close up on me now," he said with a friendly smile, "you have to play along. Stay open to me."

He put his hand to his chin, opening his mouth slightly.

"You, my friend, are also in pain. And, just like Heidi, your pain is holding you back. There is a lot of strong energy in you, but it is overshadowed."

I kept a blank expression, but inside, my mind was racing.

He doesn't know about my knee. There's no way. I haven't even felt pain this whole ride! Don't say my knee. Don't say my knee.

"Aha!" He proclaimed, "you have Erectile Dysfunction!"

I froze, my jaw dropped open, unsure of whether to celebrate that he was wrong (*wait, he is wrong, right? I function normal, don't I?*) or to be offended. But, after just a half-second, he smiled to let me know he was just kidding. I laughed uncontrollably for a few seconds, and he did too.

"You're hilarious," I said sarcastically.

"I'm just messing with you, brother."

He paused and I looked for a comfortable opening to press him for the truth about his trick. I pulled over to the curb in front of his building and prepared to call him to the carpet, but he opened his door before I had the chance.

He swung his door open wide and placed both feet on the sidewalk, ready to eject. It was now or never.

"Amal," I began, "you owe me an explanation."

He stood next to the car, placed his right hand on the roof, and ducked his head down far enough to make eye contact.

"My friend," he said with a wry smile, "just let me know when you're ready for me to heal your right knee."

He shut the door before I could respond. The final curtain to his performance.

PART 3 - FIRE

Fire is nothing, really.
Carbon dioxide, water vapor, nitrogen, and oxygen.
Just some gases bumping into each other.
It's what you do with it that matters.

The tiniest spec of the Sun's fire left its home five-hundred
    seconds ago and just landed on your skin. It gives us
    warmth. Health. Life.
Photons have traveled for hundreds of thousands of years,
    from every corner of our galaxy to light up your night sky
    with constellations.
Fires pushed the cargo plane through the sky at 800 km/h
    that brought you this thing that you're holding.

Humans are nothing, really.
Hydrogen, carbon, nitrogen, and oxygen.
Just some cells bumping into each other.

In the last hour, fifty-seven lives were saved by medical
    professionals.
In the last year, humans donated more than 100-million pints
    of blood to needy strangers.
Every day humans create art, share parts of themselves,
    defend justice and the defenseless, instigate change for the
    better, heal from every kind of pain, find a way to pull off
    the seemingly impossible, remain faithful, overcome
    adversity, survive the unimaginable, and hold onto hope
    in the midst of darkness.

Your life is nothing, really.
Sleeping, eating, working, playing.
One eighty or ninety-year shooting star among billions.
It's what you do with it that matters.

MAGIC

Miranda stood outside Cafe Mox feeling euphoric, waiting for her ride. She could see her breath vapor, illuminated by the streetlamp above her, but the cold couldn't dampen her mood. Headlights appeared a few blocks up the street and a car approached. She slipped her worn, army-green backpack off her shoulders and re-checked her phone.

As her Uber driver pulled up and she hopped in the backseat, tossing her backpack next to her, the driver smiled a greeting.

"How was Cafe Mox tonight," he asked.

"It was great."

"Is it busy in there? Seems like a cool spot to hang out."

"I guess so. Most people hang out in the bar, I think. Our Magic Meetup group was over in the board game store part. We were the only people on that side."

The driver looked at Miranda quizzically. "Magic Meetup Group? Like magic shows and illusions?"

"No, Magic the Gathering. It's kind of like a strategy card game."

"Ohh, magic *cards*! Yeah, I've heard of that. So, you meet up with other people to play Magic?"

"Yea, every Thursday."

"That's cool. How long have you been playing?"

Miranda said, "Almost my whole life. Like since fourth grade."

The driver looked confused. "This group has been meeting up since the fourth grade?"

"Oh… no, not the group," she said, "I thought you meant how long have I been playing Magic."

"Ahh, I gotcha," he shot back, happy they'd gotten on the same page. "So how long have you been playing with this group at the bar?"

"I think I've been coming for the last month or two maybe?! Like five or six weeks. I just moved to Seattle."

The driver nodded his head with exaggerated motion, making sure Miranda could see it around his headrest.

"That's pretty awesome, then. To find some people that quickly to hang out with. I bet that's been really helpful being new in town and all."

Miranda smiled. He had no idea.

"Yeah, that's for sure. This group has saved my life. They're basically my new family."

She thought about her family back in Cottage Grove, Minnesota, worrying about her, wondering where she'd run off to. Or maybe not wondering. Maybe not even caring at all.

"That's wonderful," he said, "maybe I'll have to learn this magic card game." Miranda could tell by the twinkle in his eye that there was some honesty in his quip.

She thought back to her childhood and her first exposure to Magic the Gathering.

"No son of mine is going to play those queer games, Matthew. I don't want to see those things in my house again, do you hear?!"

Miranda was nine and still going by the name Matthew. Laying on the living room carpet, she spread out the eight cards her classmate Brett had given her in exchange for seventy-five cents and two Oreo's during recess that morning. She didn't know if a Flowstone Shambler was valuable or how an enchantment card worked, but she was mesmerized by it all. The artwork on each card. The creative names and descriptions.

Her dad, Chuck, was not pleased. To him, every decision to be made, every ethical question to be answered, came down to a few simple rules. Remain a faithful Lutheran, protect the family legacy, and represent traditional Minnesotan values. And so, if his son Matthew started showing signs of weakness, or turned out soft, that failure would fall on him as a father.

Matthew was supposed to end up playing winger for the Park High School varsity hockey team, not casting spells and summoning creatures, so Matthew had to keep this new hobby a secret. She would earn five dollars each week as daily chores yielded Saturday's allowance, and every Sunday she asked Brett to meet her in the boy's restroom after Sunday School to exchange those dollars for additional Magic the Gathering cards. Matthew kept her Bible in a navy-blue zip-up Bible cover, which had a secret pocket inside the back flap. It was perfect for MTG smuggling and Brett was a faithful dealer, whose silence was continually paid for in mint flavored Tic-Tac's. The two-dollar net profit he was making off Matthew's weekly purchases didn't hurt either.

After church, Matthew's family would make the weekly ten-minute drive up to a poorly run diner called North Pole, where Matthew would sit quietly as her two older brothers would discuss the highs and lows of the NHL season and beg Chuck to take them to the next Minnesota Wild home game. Her mind would be elsewhere, strategizing how to use her new Goblin Chariot or Karplusan Yeti. Every once in a while, her dad would ask her opinion about puck possession or one of her brothers would try to involve Matthew in their conversation, but she had learned to find a quick exit. She wanted so badly for her dad to want to talk to her, to be seen the same as his other sons; but hockey never piqued her interest and every attempt at an answer came with teasing from her brothers.

Matthew hated everything about hockey. She was forced to play on the city team every winter after turning six, and it was absolute hell. Her mom knew it, too, and two weeks into her sixth-grade season, her mom had finally seen enough and approached her husband about it.

"Chuck, he's not like our other boys," Cathy begged, "he's different. If Matthew doesn't want to play hockey, then he shouldn't have to."

"Look, if my father had let me quit something every time a coach chewed me out, I never would've become the man I am. You don't think I ever came off the ice crying? You don't think I ever tried to get my mom to talk to Dad and let me quit?! We're not raising him to be a quitter."

Matthew watched Cathy brush off the accusation of collusion and press on, determined to protect her son.

"Chuck… Matthew didn't ask me to talk to you. This is me asking. I've been at his practices. I've seen the way his teammates treat him. I've seen how much he hates it. He's only out there because he knows you want him to play. Why don't we let him pursue something else?"

When her dad sat her down and gave her the good news, Matthew was torn. She knew this was a pivotal moment in her relationship with her parents.

If she quit hockey, it felt like she also would have to give up on ever earning her father's love; but she didn't know if she could suffer through another season of hazing, verbal abuse, and punishment drills for poor play and "not being as tough as the other boys." And besides, this was the beginning of something with her mom. Cathy had seen her for who she was and then fought for her. Matthew wanted to honor that fight.

She quit hockey the next day and never looked back. She also watched her parents closely over the next few years, and saw her mom grow more and more sympathetic to the ways her son was different from other kids.

Matthew wondered if she could trust that sympathy. What would happen if those differences ever grew to a point that scared Cathy? At what point would she flip on her son and retreat to her safe hiding place behind her husband?

Just to be safe, Matthew decided to try and keep all her secrets hidden from both her parents, although she suspected that her mom knew some things. At first, it was just her MTG card collection. There had only been one other occasion, since the fateful day on the living room floor, when Chuck had seen her with any cards, and his reaction confirmed Matthew's fears.

A few cards had fallen out of a pocket onto the couch. Chuck tore them into pieces and tossed them in the air like confetti. He was making a point. It wasn't just that he didn't want his son collecting these unfamiliar, less-than-masculine and useless cards. It was that his authority as a father and the head of the house was being brought into question. He had been disobeyed. His orders defied. To Matthew, it felt like *she* had been the one torn to pieces. She knew she needed to create a system to keep her secrets out of view.

Throughout all of middle school, Matthew kept building her MTG card collection, and every school day during study hall, she'd sit in the southeast corner of room 208, pull a black three-ring binder labeled "**M**ath & **T**ri**G**" from her backpack, and play Magic with Brett, Danielle, and sometimes Alex. Inside the binder she kept a few math worksheets that were half-finished to keep up the ruse, but behind the worksheets were twenty clear plastic sleeves, each with nine baseball card sized pockets. After filling every pocket with two cards, one facing each direction, Matthew had 360 cards ready at all times to create a deck from.

In addition to the binder, Matthew also moved her clandestine deals with Brett from church to the cafeteria on Mondays. As her allowance grew, she was eventually able to purchase entire packs of cards through Brett each week. It didn't take long for her MTG collection to outgrow her binder, so she created second and third binders, labeled "**M**odern Ar**T** **G**raphics" and "**C**he**M**is**T**ry & **G**eometry." One binder stayed in her backpack at all times, while the other two were tucked away deep in her bedroom closet. Her secret was safe.

★ ★ ★ ★ ★

They'd driven twenty blocks by now, but Miranda's driver was still asking questions about Magic the Gathering.

"I've actually never even seen a Magic card," he said, "what are they like?"

"Here, I'll show you," she replied, unzipping her backpack.

Miranda still used binders for her cards. She was meticulous about her organizational system, keeping every card in its place based on rarity, card type, or how much she liked it. She grabbed the thick binder she'd brought tonight, opened it to the first sleeve and slid the top right card out of its pocket to show the driver.

It was an Oreskos Swiftclaw, a simple creature card with a power of three and toughness of one; but the picture was striking. A lion head on a warrior's body, the cat warrior wore a blue and red tunic and carried a battle-axe, crouched and ready to strike. The artist had drawn this creature in some tall grass between two mountains and the way they'd done the lighting made it look like a photograph during the late afternoon, when the sun's golden hue turns everything magical.

Miranda had always appreciated the images on MTG cards, and showing this one to the driver took her back to high school and her favorite card of all - the Elvish Champion creature card.

"I don't understand why you love that card so much, Matty, it's kind of lame. I mean, it's low manna, but also like no power or toughness… it's not a rare card. I don't get it!"

Brett was watching Matthew, who went by "Matty" at school, spinning her favorite MTG card on the cafeteria table. They were in their usual seats, four tables up the far-right side, positioned as far as possible from the tables where the hockey players sat, trying to keep a low profile as they discussed the strengths and weaknesses of different cards and deck strategies.

"I don't know," she lied, "I guess there's just something sentimental about it. It was one of my first cards."

Matty knew exactly why she loved the Elvish Champion. It was because of the artwork. The elf warrior pictured wore a form-fitting dark green breastplate, and their grayish white skin showed between the brown protective padding over their lower legs, forearms, and shoulders. Their dark red hair was pulled into a fifteen-foot-long ponytail that blew in the wind behind them, and they were armed with a spear in their right hand and finger-claws on their left. The artist had intentionally drawn the champion without a clear gender, giving them small breasts and lipstick, but also broad shoulders and well-defined muscles. If you had to choose between male and female, you'd probably lean female; but that was the wonderful thing about MTG for Matty - these creatures weren't of this world. They were something else. An escape from the monotonous, boring life presented to her. And even though she didn't fully understand why at the time, Matty had loved the Elvish Champion from the first time she saw it. More than that, she wanted to *be* the Elvish Champion.

However, sitting in the Park High School cafeteria six weeks before the end of their sophomore year, Matty was not ready to confide in her best friend just yet. It wasn't that she didn't trust him. They had been best friends for as long as she could remember, and it was Brett who had kept her MTG secrets all along. It was just that Matty knew that her feelings about her gender and identity were intertwined with her feelings about Brett.

The two of them had been inseparable since they'd become friends in Mrs. Godwyn's first grade class. They sat together at lunch every day, joined the same extra-curricular activities, and would spend as much time as possible outside of school together, whether it was church youth activities or playing MTG at each other's house.

Even throughout middle school, as their bodies had started changing and Matty could sense a gap forming between herself and Brett, they stayed loyal. Brett started playing basketball. Matty would watch from the bleachers. Brett started growing facial hair. Matty told him how mature he looked. She felt safe with Brett. He never called her names like most of the other kids. *Faggot. Pussy.*

No matter how far he drifted back to center, back to "normal," he still wanted to be Matty's best friend. The problem was that she wanted more than that. Matty was falling in love with Brett. Every time he'd describe Erica Swanson's perfect butt or how he wanted to ask out Christina Kline and "go on dates with her new double-D twins," Matty would smile and nod, imagining Brett talking about her that way.

Meanwhile, as much as Matty was falling for Brett, she was also learning to hate her own body. With every new development that puberty brought, she felt more disgusted and strangely disconnected from herself. She would give anything to be free from her stupid skin and to jump into a body that looked more like the Elvish Champion. And sitting in the cafeteria, spinning her favorite card, she decided that she would become the Elvish Champion. Or at least her own version of it. And so, she did what she could.

Matty started by shaving the fuzz that grew in her armpits, and she would have shaved her face and legs if she had needed to. Fortunately, she was nearly hairless. She wore the smallest, tightest underwear she could find, thinking it might help keep her penis from fully developing. Everything about her penis was wrong. It felt like an extra limb that didn't belong.

One day in the gym locker room she had heard Scott Nelson say that Tighty-Whities stop erections. It was worth a shot.

During the summer before eleventh grade, Matty had an epiphany. From her earliest moments, Matty was different from all the boys she knew. It felt like she had nothing in common with them. After puberty, she felt attracted to men. She loved Brett and wanted to be with him, and she also hated her body and desperately wanted a different one. The answer was simple.

She was a woman.

Over time, the profound clarity of this idea sank in. It was obvious now. She had always been a woman. Matty knew it as solidly as she knew anything. Over the next twelve months, she researched everything she could about transitioning genders and started making changes. She started small. One quarter of the suggested dose of estrogen, and every other day instead of daily. Girl's panties instead of briefs, but only on days she didn't have gym class. Women's deodorant that smelled basically the same as her old stick. But, with each passing month, Matty found more strength. More resolve.

As she stepped further into womanhood, she also devised smarter systems for keeping her secrets safe in her bedroom closet. She started taking full estrogen doses every day, keeping the pills hidden in the bottom of a tackle-box, which she had otherwise filled with fishing gear. Three shoeboxes labeled "baseball cards" housed her full wardrobe of bras and panties, which she was now wearing under every outfit and washing at the laundromat behind Burger King. And the sneakiest solution of all - her collection of Sports Illustrated magazines. Her parents wouldn't think anything of her sudden interest in sports, and she could ogle the physique of world-class athletes. The four pictures of Brett from last summer's pool party that she'd cropped with scissors always stayed tucked away inside the bottom-most magazine.

Matty hadn't felt so alive and full of purpose since she first discovered Magic the Gathering. She would wake up every morning with newfound enthusiasm. She found herself smiling a lot and singing to herself. She spent hours alone in her room, listening through her dad's vinyl collection of eighties rock albums, which he had force-fed her since she was a toddler. She felt connected to Freddie Mercury and Elton John, and belted out their lyrics, while checking and re-checking her closet-vault of secrets. Life was good and everything was running smoothly. Everything except Brett. He was still falling head over heels for everyone not named Matty.

Then, three days before their Senior year started, Brett texted her and suggested they go to Applebee's for lunch and then go see a movie - their regular summer activities. Reading the text, however, Matty knew she couldn't hold everything in anymore. She felt like she would literally explode. So, she decided it was time to tell Brett everything.

Driving the family Honda Odyssey to Applebee's, her heart thundering in her chest, Matty imagined bringing her MTG card collection to life, summoning a Tidal Kraken for its power and a Yawgmoth Demon for its toughness. Arming herself with the right spells and manna-producing artifacts. If only the fantasy world she'd spent so much time with could help her now. Out here, in this realm, she felt powerless and vulnerable. Unprepared and defenseless. Unsure of what strategies to use or how to react if Brett unleashed an attack.

Shaking and petrified, she walked into Applebee's and sank into their favorite booth in the back right corner. She laid out all the tokens of her life on the table. Props to help her tell her story. The Elvish Champion card. Black lace underwear. Her favorite photo of Brett sunbathing shirtless next to the Milano's backyard pool. A server came over with a glass of water and glanced over the table quizzically. Matty didn't even notice. Brett was all that mattered now. She was about to place her whole life in his hands.

Matty saw him striding into the restaurant, swinging the door wide and walking with the confidence of this year's most likely homecoming king. He looked perfect. Dark blue designer jeans. The ones with rips and holes pre-made. White long-sleeve t-shirt that was last year's basketball warm-up shirt. His blonde hair parted on the left and held firm in a messy wave by the non-shiny hair gel. Eighteen freckles running across his cheeks and nose (Matty had counted them a few times).

Brett gave Matty his signature half-smile and nod as he approached the booth. She beamed back, warmth flashing through her entire body. And for a second, she completely forgot all about her secrets and her plan and the potential for life-wrecking rejection. It was only her and Brett that existed. Just the way she liked it.

"What's all this," Brett asked as he slid into his seat opposite Matty. "Lost and found?"

Matty was yanked out of her dream-state and thrust back into reality. She took a deep breath.

"Here goes everything," she thought. Then she spoke.

Over seventeen minutes and twenty-six seconds, she told Brett everything.

It was the last time Brett ever spoke to her.

Miranda's driver was bringing up other card games, asking if MTG was similar to any of them.

She chuckled. "Not really. Magic the Gathering is pretty unique."

"I guess I'll just have to try it sometime," he said.

"Yeah."

Miranda pressed her forehead against the window glass, happy to be a passenger. She hated driving at night. They were cutting through downtown, passing through blocks of buildings all lit up. As she felt the high beams of oncoming cars gliding across her face like searchlights, Miranda was transported back to the last time she ever drove at night. Back to the worst night of her life.

The thinnest, shiniest snowflakes were slowly drifting down from the clouds, melting almost as soon as they made contact with her windshield. The headlights moving north on Route Ten each transitioned from muted yellow to hot white, blinding Matty for a split-second, and then to a blurry orange as they glided past. Matty normally treated this weekly thirty-minute drive home from Town House Bar as her own private karaoke session, an encore performance without any drag, singing along to the eighties rock anthems on KOOL 107.9FM. But tonight, the radio was off and Matty's hands had a death-grip on the steering wheel.

The night had gone fine, as usual. Same conversations with Tiffany, the bartender who organized the shows and looked the other way that Matty was only eighteen. She'd given a typical performance on stage - tonight's song of choice was Madonna's *Into the groove*. Normal food and drink order - Chicken Strips and a Dr. Pepper. But something was bothering her. Nagging at her sense of safety. Like that one night four months ago when she saw Phil Cranston, her old Sunday School teacher, in the audience and had to bail on the whole show.

As she exited off Route Ten onto 80th Street, Matty replayed the whole night in her mind, trying to find what was wrong. Nothing stuck out to her, but she knew something was off. She turned left onto 80th and tried to slow her breathing. She ran through her Saturday night drive home checklist, hoping that would calm her down. Changed back into jeans and very boyish t-shirt. Check. Removed wig and all jewelry, stashing it in the small duffel bag under the van's back seat. Check. Wiped off all makeup and gave herself one brief spray of Axe body spray. Check. See? Nothing was wrong. Everything was going to be fine.

But then, as she approached the fire station and looked to the right, she noticed it. Brett's car, normally parked just off 80th on Innsdale Avenue, across the street from his house, was gone. Brett was never out on a Saturday night, especially at 11:45pm. But then, forty-five seconds later, as she turned onto Jensen Avenue, Matty's heart sank. Brett's car was in her driveway. This was DEFCON level two. The one person who knew all her secrets, who was no longer speaking to her, who could ruin her life… was at her house. Matty decided to circle the block a few times while she tried to hatch a plan.

Walking in the front door, Matty looked to the right and scanned the living room floor. Here, where everything had started years earlier, every secret she'd held dear had been brought out of her bedroom closet and was spread out, like incriminating evidence for the jury to see. Three binders flung open and several MTG cards strewn about. A shoebox of women's underwear and bras laying open on its side. The Sports Illustrated magazines torn and wrinkled, with the printed photos of Brett, once hidden inside the oldest issue, resting on top of the pile. Pill bottles lined up neatly in front of the tackle-box that once kept them hidden. Someone had taken the time to align the bottles, so the labels faced Matty perfectly, and they were in alphabetical order. Estrogen, Progestin, and Spironolactone. She wondered if her mom had gone and looked them up. Matty hadn't even tried to cover the bottle's labels, knowing that if her parents ever opened the tackle-box, she'd be in hot water no matter what pills they thought were inside.

Her gaze stayed low, staring at the contents of her closet, framed in by Brett's Adidas, her mom's slippers, and Chuck's dress socks. And even in that moment, knowing that they had all abandoned her, knowing they'd betrayed her, knowing they were the ones in the wrong; she was overwhelmed by guilt and self-hatred. She had failed to destroy her weird inner self. She hadn't been able to become the kind of young man that could earn their love. And she hated herself for it, even more than she hated them that night.

Over the next forty-eight minutes, Matty's life was torn apart, piece by piece, by the three people she loved the most. The people she desperately wanted love from. Sitting on the floor, weeping in silence, the lump in her throat grew larger and larger. Breathing became harder and harder. She wanted to explain. To tell them she was sorry she couldn't be the son or best friend they wanted. To share in their hatred for the woman she was becoming. Maybe they would accept her then. Maybe they could still love her if she could just get the words out.

Finally, Matty heard a throaty whisper crawl out of her body, wondering who was choosing her words.

"Dad… Mom… I'm not your son anymore. I'm your daughter and my name is Miranda."

The panic attack that had been coming on slowly, became a hurricane-like force inside her, pushing Miranda into the fetal position. She felt vomit pooling around her. Chuck was still stammering away loudly. Cathy had left the room moaning. Brett was staring at everyone else, open-mouthed. Miranda surrendered to the internal storm until her eyes closed shut and the noise of their vitriol faded away.

The next morning, Miranda's eyelids eased open, and she pushed herself up onto her elbows, taking in her surroundings. She was in a hospital room and according to the clock on the salmon-colored concrete block walls, it was just past eleven on Sunday. She guessed she was on the second floor, based on the view out the silver metal window that looked like it hadn't been opened in decades. On the wall opposite her there was a small dry-erase board with "Matthew M." written on it. Her mother's doing, no doubt.

After a few minutes, a middle-aged nurse with the resting scowl of a diner waitress peered in the window that made up most of the door's top-half. Seeing Miranda awake, she pushed the door open just wide enough to poke her head in the door.

"Good afternoon sleepy-head," she said, sounding annoyed, "welcome to the land of the living."

Miranda had no idea what she meant by that.

"Hi," she croaked, "is anyone here?"

"You mean your mother?"

Miranda didn't respond.

"She stopped by a few hours ago. You were still sleepin'. But she left you something." The nurse jerked her head toward the night stand next to the bed. There was a sky-blue envelope laying next to the phone. It looked like it contained a Hallmark card. Probably purchased at the gift shop in the lobby.

"Anyway," the nurse continued, "you're free to go. Clothes are in that bag right there." She widened her eyes and shifted them toward the tan plastic chair beneath the window. Miranda looked over at the bag of her clothes in the chair, then at the whiteboard, then back to the nurse.

"My name's not Matthew," she said.

"Uh huh," came the reply, as the nurse backed out of the door frame and allowed the wooden door to close.

Miranda let out a sigh and swung her legs over the side of the bed. Her puke-stained jeans and Maroon Five t-shirt stared at her judgmentally from the chair in front of her. A costume she'd used to hide under. She felt anger and hatred just looking at it. Why did she have to wear a costume at all? Why couldn't she just be Miranda instead of pretending to be Matthew? And yet, no matter how loud the voices of injustice and righteous anger were, she could always hear the whisper of shame, echoing from her earliest programming at home or Sunday School. She wondered if she'd ever break free of Matthew. If she'd ever feel like herself. Flinging the privacy curtain closed, Miranda changed out of the hospital gown and promised herself this would be the last time she would wear men's clothing. No more costumes. No more pretending.

The blue envelope caught her eye as she was turning to leave. She opened it, a little curious about what her mom wanted to say, but also knowing that it didn't matter. She'd already chosen her next move. She slid out the cliche 'get well soon' greeting card. Yep, definitely from the gift shop downstairs. Inside the card were five crisp one-hundred-dollar bills and a scribbled note from Cathy.

Matthew,

I've always loved you and stood up for you, no matter how different you were from our other sons. And I still love you now, but you've gone too far. I don't know why you're doing this to us, but I just want my son back. The van is parked out front and I've booked you a room at the Country Inn. Stay there a few nights to let your father cool down. And then I hope you'll come home, apologize, and reconsider your choices so we can be a family again.

Love, Mom

Miranda pocketed the cash and tossed the card in the trash can by the hospital entrance. She stopped home to fill up a few duffel bags, knowing her family would be at North Pole Diner. The living room had been transformed back to normal, all evidence of Miranda's misdeeds swept away, but it only took her six minutes to find all of her prized possessions. They'd been picked up off the carpet and dumped in the garbage bin in the garage.

She found room in her duffel bags for her MTG collection, some clothes, pills, her laptop, and a few pawnable items from around the house, and then she stopped in the kitchen to write a note back to Cathy. Then, she drove to the St. Paul Union Depot, bought a bus ticket for Seattle, and sat down to wait for her bus.

Sitting in 8D, Miranda spent the first few hours of the bus ride staring out the window at the countryside, still stunned by everything that had transpired in the last nineteen hours. It felt like her worst nightmare, and she wanted to wake up.

She'd been plotting her move to Seattle for months, ever since she read an article describing the LGBTQ-friendly neighborhoods and welcoming culture. But still, planning to move to Seattle someday was a completely different thing than impulsively packing a few bags, spending $98.32 on a bus ticket, and leaving Minnesota on her own for the first time. She had no place to stay when she got there, no job lined up, and she didn't know a single person within two-thousand miles. Her thoughts were spiraling, overwhelming her. She took a deep breath and double-checked her wallet.

There was the $500 from Mom, which after the bus ticket was down to $401.68. But Miranda wasn't too worried about finances. She'd been able to save up a few thousand dollars over the last year, working at the Starbucks inside HyVee after school. One of the perks to having your only friend abandon you and no desire to be around your own family - you find the motivation to get a job.

Oh crap. My job. Terry's expecting me to work my shift tomorrow!

As the bus pulled into Fargo, the first long stopover, Miranda called her manager to quit. She explained some of her situation and why she needed to get out of town and apologized for not being able to give more notice. Bracing for a verbal lashing, Miranda listened through Terry's response. He wasn't angry. He didn't yell. In fact, Terry praised her courage to leave and told her he'd find her a spot in one of the Starbucks locations in Seattle.

Maybe she was just exhausted after everything that had happened. Maybe she was experiencing a gesture of kindness for the first time in a while. No matter the reason, Miranda cried hard for the next thirty minutes of her bus ride. The dam that was holding all the emotion and tension of the last twenty-four hours had burst and the release felt therapeutic and healing. Eventually the tears stopped, and Miranda cleaned herself up. Then, with only thirteen hours left until her destination, she laid her head against the window and fell fast asleep.

One week after signing the lease on a cramped studio south of downtown, Miranda wrapped a nylon rope over two blades of the dusty ceiling fan, then around her neck twice, and tied it in a knot. Standing on the better of her two wooden chairs, she bent her knees, putting just enough weight on the rope to test her knot. The nylon stung her neck and the ensuing instinct to back off was stronger than she'd expected, but the knot held. She paused, and the muscles in her legs tightened, preparing to kick the chair over.

Miranda's first month in Seattle had been beyond miserable. She had traded in the snow and freezing cold for a pervasive gray that never eased up. Every day she'd go to work at the busiest coffee shop she'd ever seen, and then, exhausted, she would shuttle around town to look for apartments, in a city where she knew no one. Where she spoke to no one. She didn't even have an emergency contact to list on the lease.

And then there was the problem with her legal name. Everywhere she turned, looking to start over with a new place to live, a new doctor, a new driver's license, she was brought face to face with the life she'd fled.

Sign here: *Matthew Millford*

She remembered the hospital room and the pitiful 'get well' card from the lobby with bribe money inside.

Sign here: *Matthew Millford*

The living room carpet materialized in front of her, her precious possessions splattered across it. Her Dad's face, flush with anger.

Sign here: *Matthew Millford*

Applebee's. Corner booth. Brett's eyebrows furrowing in a mix of surprise and embarrassment over being her friend. The flaring nostrils of anger. The strawberry lemonade spilling onto her lap as he tumbled out of his seat and out of her life.

Miranda was utterly alone. Everyone had abandoned her just as soon as they saw the true person hiding in the stage wings. It seemed that no one's love could survive getting a real glimpse of her. Not even her own. She was so tired. Tired of pretending to be Matthew. Tired of the constant panic over who might discover her secrets. Tired of being alone and unloved. And most of all, tired from the never-ending battle with the inner voices of self-loathing and hatred.

She hated Matthew. She hated Matty. She hated Miranda. And she just wanted it all to go away.

Standing on the chair, nylon rope secured in place, it occurred to Miranda that she hadn't done enough planning. It takes a very specific set of moves to carry this out, and Miranda didn't have the athleticism to try it without practicing first. It was too late for that now, but she took a moment to envision each step in the process.

Step one - jump in the air to lift my weight off the chair.

Step two - kick the chair over and hope no one hears the sound and comes to check on me. Not that anyone would check on me. No one knows I even exist.

Step Three - Resist the urge to stop myself. I'm not sure how I would even do that, but it doesn't hurt to be prepared.

Ok, goodbye shitty world. You've been awful.

As soon as she jumped, Miranda's plan fell apart. The chair slid nine inches forward on liftoff and her jump changed the alignment of the rope around her neck. Her weight test did not account for the harsh impact of her body dropping from a jump. The rope slid up under her chin like a hockey helmet's chinstrap, both fan blades snapped in two, showering her with splinters, and Miranda landed hard on her tailbone, her shin cracking against the chair in front of her on the way down.

She ended up laying on her back with a large piece of a fan blade stuck into her bleeding left forearm. Her neck was on fire, and she felt a sharp pain coming from her tailbone, which she was fairly confident was fractured. And all that commotion, it turns out, can be heard by exactly three neighbors, all of whom burst into Miranda's apartment through the unlocked front door exactly thirty-eight seconds later.

Dierdre, the mid-forties psychic healer who was first on the scene, drove her to the hospital. Miranda had resisted at first, but Dierdre's presence and tone were so motherly and nurturing, she found herself accepting the help. She was drawn to Dierdre. It was obvious that Dierdre knew what had happened. She had been in situations like this before, Miranda realized. No words were said about the incident, but then again, no explanation was needed. The broken fan. The rope-burn marks on the neck. The wooden chair placed underneath the fan. It all told a pretty clear story.

Dierdre talked non-stop, filling the entire fifteen-minute trip to Harbor View Medical Center. Miranda suspected that this was on purpose, giving her the space to just process everything, and she was thankful. Each passing minute with

Dierdre helped ease Miranda's embarrassment. There was something peaceful about her that made Miranda feel safe.

An hour later, sitting on an ice pack in a hospital room, waiting to talk to a mental health professional, Miranda thought back to one thing Dierdre said.

"We're village people, whether we want to admit it or not. Birth families, chosen families, communities… something. We're not meant to be alone. Working in cubicles, living in studio apartments, keeping to ourselves. We need love. Friendship. Even enemies and exes."

Miranda had plenty of enemies and exes, sort of, but she didn't have a village. She didn't have anyone or anything positive. And in that moment, spurred on by Dierdre and perhaps energized by the relief of her survival, Miranda decided she was going to find a tribe.

She had no idea where to start until she remembered overhearing the two people sitting behind her on the bus ride to Seattle. They were roommates, who were also going to be new in town, and they were talking about their plans for making friends. They had downloaded an app called Meetup and were looking through different groups together, commenting on each one.

Even though the hospital didn't have Wi-Fi, and the concrete was limiting her data speeds, Miranda was able to download the app and started scrolling through the local groups. It didn't take long for her to find her first potential village - Magic the Gathering Meetup, every Thursday at Cafe Mox. Three days later she limped into the cafe, wearing an ankle-length forest green skirt and black blouse, both terrified and hopeful.

It was her fifth week in a row, and Miranda was starting to like the Magic Meetup group. Walking into the small room in the back of the game store felt like stepping through a portal into another world. Another universe, where Cottage Grove, Minnesota didn't exist, and Miranda had never been Matthew.

Midway through unpacking her chosen binder for the night, she looked up at Josh, the group leader, who was getting the group's attention.

"Hey everyone, we have a new person joining tonight. This is Nikko." He stepped to the left slightly and motioned with both arms toward a skinny, frightened-looking person with very curly orange hair.

Miranda recognized the fear in Nikko's face. She still felt it a little, but it was waning each week. Josh introduced the group to Nikko, walking around the table and pausing at each person.

"This is Felipe. This is Sam."

He stood right next to Miranda and smiled.

"This is Miranda, she just moved here from Minnesota… right Miranda?"

Miranda was spellbound. Her mouth wouldn't move. Frozen in shock.

Did Josh just say 'she'?!? Wait. Rewind. 'This is Miranda, SHE, just moved here…' Yep. SHE!

Just that one word - a simple pronoun - made all the difference. No one had ever referred to her as 'she' or 'her' or anything even remotely close. She choked back her tears. Her face flushed. A smile spread across her face and stayed there the whole night. She didn't care how badly she was losing in MTG. Miranda had tasted what it was like to just be Miranda. No Matthew. No Matty. No slurs or judgmental caveats. Just pure acceptance of her in all her womanhood, and it felt rapturous.

Three hours later, Miranda stood outside Cafe Mox feeling euphoric, waiting for her ride. She could see her breath vapor, illuminated by the streetlamp above her, but the cold couldn't dampen her mood. Headlights appeared a few blocks up the street and a car approached. She slipped her worn, army-green backpack off her shoulders and re-checked her phone.

While she knew that nobody else in the world could completely understand her journey, that no one could fully get what she'd been through, she hoped she'd get a chance to tell her story. To share what she'd been through with someone, somehow, someday. And then, as the car eased to a stop right in front of her and she saw her reflection in the windows - a reflection she was happy to see for the first time in her life - she had a thought that made her smile. Maybe she could start with the Uber driver.

BUTTERFLIES

My phone informed me that I'd be picking up two different passengers, headed in the same general direction, presumably. I picked up Krista first, from a hotel downtown. One of those old, classic brick buildings that was bought by some conglomerate with loads of cash. A chic downtown landmark, where they preserved the facade of the building and completely renovated the inside. A sleek, clean surprise, encased inside some old, run-down bricks.

As Krista glided out the automatic glass doors and headed toward the car, I hopped out to help her load her bright red, hard-shell roller bag into the trunk. She was short and thin, wearing black jeans, a white button-down shirt, and a gray vest over the top. She looked like a fancy caterer. She was, in fact, a software developer. A brand-new software developer fresh off her final interview with a tech company and feeling good about the offer they had extended her. She was flying home today, excited to pack up her life and move to the Northwest.

During the six minutes in traffic between Krista's hotel and Phil's apartment building, Krista told me all about her interview with this "super chill startup." Apparently, she had originally taken the interview as a practice run before trying to get into Google or Microsoft, but wound up loving the company and the team she interviewed with. This small, spunky startup was now her dream job.

As I checked the navigation, I asked her what job she'd be leaving to come out here and noticed Phil's pickup location was in an alley.

"I'd better try the street side first, in case the navigation is just off," I thought to myself as we turned onto Phil's street and Krista chatted about being between careers.

"Between careers, huh?" I asked, splitting my attention between searching for Phil and Krista's life story.

"Yeah," she said, nonchalantly, "before I got sick, I taught middle school math, but then I ended up in a coma, and after that I was in the hospital for a few months and needed something to do."

Her casual, monotone expression made it sound like she was discussing last week's dinner outing with her in-laws. I gave up my search for Phil and repeated her story back to her as questions.

"Hold on… you were a math teacher?"

"Uh huh."

"And you were in a coma? And then... just... needed something to do?!?" I added air quotes and a smile through the rear-view mirror.

She smiled back and said flatly, "yeah, basically. I had to be in a hospital bed for two months after coming out of the coma, so I figured I might as well do something besides watch PBS!"

"So, what did you do?" I probed.

"I learned Python."

I turned around in my seat and stared at her wide-eyed and smirking, blinking rapidly in cartoon-like exaggerated surprise. She giggled.

"It's a computer language," she said.

"Yeah, I know it's a computer language," I replied, still blinking.

"Well, then what?"

She knew what, but wanted me to say it.

"That's just... I don't know," I began, searching for the right adjective, "that's just unheard of, you know?"

"What is?" she asked.

"Well, it's like this. You were at a low point. Maybe the lowest point of your life, with a lot a difficult things happening it sounds like. And I don't know... but most people in situations like that have a hard enough time just trying to deal with all of that, you know?"

I paused and she nodded, giving me a half-smile.

"I'm just impressed, I guess... that you were in a hospital, recovering from a coma and stuff, and were still able to be positive and learn computer programming."

"Thanks," she replied, smiling in a way that made it seem like she was grateful someone noticed.

We sat in silence for a moment, the meaningfulness of the interaction sinking in. I wanted to ask more about her sickness and the coma, but I wasn't sure how to bring it up. Twice I inhaled quickly, preparing to start a question, and then bailed at the last second. Krista must've sensed my questions, because she answered them before I could figure out how to ask them.

"It was a brain tumor," she said, "the thing that caused the coma. I passed out in the middle of a lesson one day at school and they did a bunch of tests on me. Nothing came up on the tests, so they kept me overnight for observation and my body started shutting down. I was in a coma for eleven days, and they found the tumor on day three."

"Wow," was all I could say. I wanted to say more. To express how awful it sounded and how sorry I was that she had to go through that, and how evil it is that brain tumors even exist, and things like that.

And just as I was opening my mouth to stumble through something along those lines, the passenger door opened, and the sounds of the city cut me off.

Phil was in his mid-fifties, tall with broad shoulders, and had the longest beard I had seen on a real person in my life. His greasy, gray hair was pulled back into a ponytail and he was sporting work boots, cargo shorts, and an orange t-shirt with more stains on it than the shirts I turn into cleaning rags.

"Pick up for Phil, right?" His voice was both scratchy and full. Santa Claus with a smoking habit.

"Uh, yeah," I stammered, turning back around in my seat. It felt like I had just awakened from a dream. Phil was already buckled in.

"All present and accounted for," he announced and tossed his head around to face Krista and gave her a wave.

"Hello there, are you headed to the airport, too?"

"Hi," Krista said, "Yeah, gotta catch a flight to Kansas City."

"Kansas City," Phil sang back to her, drawing out the word Kansas, "Fine city. Good people."

There was no response needed. He was just stating facts.

"Have you ever been?" Krista asked.

"Oh sure," Phil responded, "but it's been a while. Last time I was there would've been the late eighties or so."

"Huh." Krista's voice trailed off. She seemed deep in thought. "You seem really familiar to me. I can't place it, but I feel like I've seen you before."

"It's probably Linda's," he said.

"Who's Linda?"

"Linda's Tavern. I bartend there."

Krista was confused. "What? No, I've never been to Linda's Tavern. This is my first time in Seattle."

Phil shifted slightly in his seat to get a better look at Krista.

"Well, I don't know what to tell 'ya then," he offered, "maybe I remind you of someone you know."

My two passengers seemed about as different from each other as two people could be. I was sure they had nothing in common, which was going to make conversation difficult. A few awkward seconds passed, and I tried to think of a strategy to ease the discomfort. I decided to share Krista's coma story with Phil, but I wasn't sure if that was something she wanted me to make public, so I fumbled through a few words, hoping she would take over. She started to, but she had barely gotten a sentence out before Phil interrupted with the force of a locomotive.

"We're coma buddies?!" He was smiling at Krista, revealing crooked, yellow teeth.

"In fact," he continued, "that's probably where you recognize me from."

Krista, frozen in place, seemed as confused as I was at what that meant, as Phil continued.

"When was your coma? Last year?"

"Um, what? Yeah," she stammered, "yeah, August."

Phil seemed pleased with himself for guessing it.

"Yep, I thought so. Mine was July twenty-seventh to September third."

Krista was speechless. I was not.

"Hold on," I said, "Phil, you were in a coma too?"

"Sure was!"

"And you two were in a coma... what? At the same time?"

"That's right!"

I whistled through my teeth. Krista was still frozen.

"I mean... what are the odds?!"

As this incredible coincidence sunk in, I suddenly felt an urge to seize the moment. I felt like I was observing something amazing, like an interstellar cosmic event. Something I needed to get the details of and record for future generations. In my mind, I saw myself setting up my telescope and flattening the pages of my journal. Touching the end of my pen to my tongue.

"So, what was it like," I asked to no one in particular, "coming out of a coma?"

Phil prepared to answer, but I realized it might be rude of me to ask strangers about the details of their past traumatic events, so I added a caveat, secretly hoping they'd ignore it.

"I mean, only if it's something you're comfortable talking about."

Krista stayed silent. A deer in headlights. Phil took off like a racehorse out of the gate.

"Coming out of the coma is a little odd, that's for sure. It can be totally different for different people, you know; but, for me it was a slow, drug-filled journey. Just like my cross-country road trip in the late sixties!"

He paused and grinned at his own joke.

"No, but seriously it's kind of like waking from really deep sleep. Like coming back from one of those dreams where you're still not sure what's real and what's not, you know?"

"Uh huh," I offered, wondering if I had possibly overestimated this moment.

"Because that's the thing," Phil continued, "you're not asleep in a coma. You're conscious. Totally awake the whole time. And that's the fun part."

I was at a loss for words. It wasn't that Phil's revelation contradicted what I thought about comas. I hadn't ever really thought about what the experience was like for the person in a coma, but sleep seemed to be the closest experience I knew of. But even then, it shouldn't have been all that surprising to hear that you're conscious in a coma. But it was. I was astounded.

I glanced in the rear-view mirror to try and get a sense of Krista's perspective on all this. Would she confirm what Phil was saying? Add to it? Her face showed no change. Mouth still open, eyes looking vaguely in Phil's direction. Meanwhile, Phil kept rolling along.

"Yeah, that's the thing most people don't get - you're not asleep. No sir. You're conscious. Well, that's not the right word. It's more like you're dreaming. Because you're awake, I guess you could say, but not awake too. At least, not awake the way you're probably thinking."

"Huh," I said, trying to think of other types of being awake.

"Right," Phil said, speaking slower now, "it's more like… like you're somewhere else. I guess, sort of like being transported or something."

"Somewhere else?"

"Yeah, like another space. Or maybe transported to another… what's the word?"

"Planet?" I offered, looking back and forth between the two of them.

Phil looked at the ceiling. Krista continued staring at nothing.

"Not planet…" Phil said, "another… hang on it's on the tip of my throat…"

I waited, without correcting his idiom.

"Dimension!" he shouted, "it's like being in another dimension."

This was going to get interesting. He was adding a sequel to *A Wrinkle in Time*, while Krista looked as if she were slipping into another coma in my back seat.

"Tell me about this other dimension," I said. And so, he did.

"Well, first of all," Phil began, "you're sitting in this giant field. Er, it's not a field really, but there's just this perfect grass for as far as you can see left and right. I'd say it's as wide as a football field or so. Yeah, pretty wide, but stretching out farther than you can see in both directions. Oh, and the grass isn't green, it's orange."

"Orange?" I checked.

"Yeah, like a dark orange. But definitely grass. Super soft, thick, perfect grass. It wasn't itchy or rough at all, you know? The kind of grass they'd have at the Governor's mansion."

I raised my eyebrows and nodded, as if to say, "that sounds pretty nice!"

"Right, so you're sitting in this perfect orange grass, and there's people everywhere. Well, not everywhere. Not like a crowd or anything. Everyone is spread out, in small groups. For example, I was in a group of three for most of the time, with Paulo and Irene. And then, just before I left, Laura joined our group. But you could see a handful of groups spread around the general area.

I kept nodding, not wanting to interrupt.

"OK, and then in front of you is this river-thing, separating you from the other side."

"River-thing?"

"Yeah," he said, "it's like a river, but it's not water. Clouds are the water. Puffy, silver clouds rushing past at probably forty miles per hour. And all the clouds put together are so thick, you can't get a glimpse of what's below, or how deep it is."

"Did you get in the river," I asked, "or reach into it?"

Phil shook his head.

"No, you can't touch the river. It's too far down from the bank. You just look at it. But that river was so calming. So comforting. I would just stare at it for hours and listen to its sound."

He turned to look at me and said, "It would sort of hum. Like a fan or a prop-plane engine or something like that. And it felt like the sound was surrounding you. Like it was coming from inside of you, you know? Oh my god, I loved that river so much, man!"

Phil's chuckle morphed into a brief coughing fit, before settling down. He stared out the window. I didn't want him to stop or lose his place in the story.

"So, there was the orange grass and the cloud river," I summarized, "and what was on the other side of the river?"

Phil became serious, almost.

"That's the thing," he said, "I don't know! Most of the other side was blocked by tall, black hedge bushes. At least, I think they were hedge bushes. That's what they looked like. They were about fifteen feet tall I'd say, and too thick to see through, so there's no telling what was on the other side. But then, there were these gaps in the hedges where the bridges were, and we would all try to see in the gaps, you know? But it was weird, because all you could see was light. It was a bright glowing light. It was definitely coming from inside the black hedges, but it was too bright to see what it was or anything, even if we shielded our eyes."

As Phil described everything, my mind took me there. It felt like I could see everything he was describing. Almost an out of body experience. My physical self was still driving them to the airport, but this other part of me had traveled to this coma-dimension and was trying to look into the hedges.

"That sounds surreal," I said, immediately feeling awkward for phrasing it that way, but bumbling on anyway. "I mean, like I know it's not 'real'... ... but not that your experience isn't real to you or anything. I'm not trying to say you're making this up or something like that."

I exhaled violently, hoping any other insensitive and demeaning words might slide out of my head with the carbon dioxide.

"Did you say there were bridges?" I asked.

"Oh yes," Phil responded, graciously ignoring my rude assessment of his story's truthfulness, "didn't I tell you about the bridges?"

"No. Well, I mean, you just mentioned them now..."

"Oh, how did I forget the bridges!?"

I gave him a half-chuckle and he returned it, and then he jumped back in with full enthusiasm.

"Every so often along the river... I'd say every one-hundred-fifty-yards or so, there would be a bridge that connected the two sides. They were these giant stone bridges.

Probably forty feet wide and each side of the path on top had these little stone walls, like guardrails for the bridge. And they had flowers and plants growing in the cracks between the stones. They were curved bridges - arches, you know, with vines hanging down in the middle. All these vines, like maybe thirty of them, just hanging off the sides and the bottom of the bridge. And some of the vines were so long, the ends would disappear down into the clouds in the river. And every bridge lined up straight to one of those gaps in the hedges, you know, like I told you, where you'd see that golden glow coming from inside."

"Wow," I said, impressed with the level of detail in his descriptions, "I feel like I can see the bridges in my mind."

"Phil," I continued, "this leads me to my next question…
…did you ever try and cross over a bridge to the other side?"

"Almost," he said as if he knew this question was coming, "I don't know, there was this thing where you could just kind of sense where you were supposed to be. I don't want to be cheesy, but it was like I knew it wasn't my time yet to cross over."

"Mmm," I said, indicating my acknowledgment without interrupting.

"But there was a time toward the end when I almost went out on the bridge," he said. "I just felt this pull inside, drawing me to the bridge. Trying to get me to go across. But then, there was another feeling, like an inner-voice I guess you could say, that was pulling me back."

"That's incredible," I offered, "was that right before you woke up?"

"Pretty much!"

"Wow. So, at the end of the time. Wait Phil, how long were you in a coma for again?"

"Five and a half weeks"

"Ok, five and a half weeks," I repeated, "So did it feel like that long in this other dimension? Did you sleep at night? Eat meals? Did you do anything other than just talk to each other?"

"No, it wasn't like that."

"What do you mean? It wasn't like what?"

"We didn't sleep or eat or anything like that."

"Oh, so you just talked all day with your group?"

"You could say that. But there wasn't really day and night. Not like here. There was just time."

"Time?"

"Yeah, time. Just some amount of time went by. I never really thought about how long it was, to be honest with 'ya. It was five and a half weeks, I suppose. But I'd say, to my brain, it was like a day."

"A day? Just one day?"

"Well, yeah. But it felt longer than a day. It just didn't have any nighttime or any way to make it seem like we were moving to day two or something. So, it just felt like a long day. We had different conversations, and we'd explore the bridge areas and the riverbank, but it just all happened in one long day."

"That's so fascinating," I said.

"Yea, I suppose the one time when I thought about time was just after Laura joined our group, because I thought about how we needed to catch her up on everything that had happened. Right toward the end."

"Uh huh. So, right before the time you almost crossed the bridge and then you woke up?"

"Yes sir."

I thought about that for a moment. I was enamored with Phil's story. It was incredible and I was hanging on every detail he shared.

"So do you think crossing the bridge would've been like-?" I couldn't say the word.

"It would've been death," he said. "No question about it."

"Whew. Well, I'm really glad you didn't cross the bridge then!"

He laughed in agreement.

"But you want to know the crazy thing? After I woke up, after the drugs wore off and I could think straight, you want to know what my first thought was?! I wanted to go back! I didn't really worry about the death part of it. I just kept thinking how much I missed that place, whatever it was. The grass on my skin. The humming of the river. The conversation with my group…"

Phil trailed off and turned to look out the window again, no doubt transporting himself back to his coma-location in his mind. Then, Krista broke her silence.

"And the butterflies. Don't forget about the big purple butterflies."

Phil whipped around, his eyes wide in surprise.

"That's right! How in the flying hell did I forget about the purple butterflies!?!" He shouted, laughing jovially. Turning back to face me, he filled me in on the butterflies.

"Yeah, so, the only animals that were there were these huge purple butterflies. I mean huge. Probably five feet long, with giant wings. And they were absolutely stunning. They had faces, which was a little weird I thought, but you kind of just get used to it. I mean, they were nice faces. Smiling. Calm. And they would just fly around above our heads, maybe twenty to thirty feet in the air, and sometimes they'd land in the grass, not too far away from us."

After a moment of limbo, he remembered another butterfly fact.

"Oh! And they sang!" Shouting again. "Not like human singing, but definitely some sort of singing. I don't really know how to describe it. What do you think? How would you say it?" He was asking Krista.

She looked at the car ceiling for a second. "I'd say it was like they had accordions inside them. Or keyboards maybe," she said, coolly. As if she hadn't been in a trance throughout the whole conversation.

"Yes, exactly!" Phil agreed, "like keyboards. Beautiful, flying, animal keyboard butterflies."

Thoughts were swirling around my head like a tornado of their keyboard-butterflies. Phil's description of this place was stunning enough, but then to try and wrap my head around the fact that Krista somehow knew about this place, presumably from her own coma?! And that she remembered the butterflies?! I couldn't make sense of it all. How did Krista know about the butterflies? Were they somehow in the same *dimension*? Were more people there? Did everyone who was ever in a coma go there? Was it related to the afterlife somehow? I didn't even know where to begin.

"Ok, so... let me get this straight," I began, "I mean, this is just... I don't even understand!"

Phil agreed. "I know! Pretty crazy huh?!"

"Yeah, crazy is an understatement. I mean, Krista...? Are you saying you had a similar experience during your coma?"

Krista started nodding vigorously, her eyebrows disappearing into her bangs.

"The exact same experience. The grass, the river, the bridges, the butterflies. I was there too."

Phil's head was slowly rocking up and down, as if he'd heard this before.

"I just never..." Krista continued, "I just always thought that I was the only one. Or not that I was the only one - there were other people there, like my group."

"So, you had a group, too, like Phil was saying?"

"Yeah, Nikki and Raul. We would go on walks a lot. Just strolling down along the river, looking at all the other groups and listening to the butterflies."

"I have a question," I announced, like a cross-examining attorney strategically leading us to the truth, "your groups - that you each had - did you talk about your lives and about the fact you were in a coma? Because then you would at least know that a *few* other people were having the same experience as you, right?"

Krista looked toward the ceiling, considering how to explain this to me.

"Sort of, but not really. We shared names and we definitely got to know each other, but it was all in the present, I'd say. We didn't really talk about anything outside of our experiences there. In fact, I wasn't all that aware of being in a coma. It was like one of those dreams where you know something's a little off, but you don't completely get that you're dreaming. And, when you try to think about your life outside of that dream, you can't really remember anything."

"Wow," I said, feeling like I got it. The way she'd explained it made complete sense. "So, when you woke from your coma, you didn't really know if those were other people or just figments of your imagination, then?"

"Right. To be honest, I never imagined meeting someone with even a remotely similar experience. I thought that this was *my* experience you know?! That other people who had been in comas would have their own experiences."

She paused and looked up, locking eyes with me in the mirror.

"I just never knew there were more of us."

"Yeah, it's a funny thing," Phil bellowed out, "some folks don't remember anything from their coma, and a couple of people I talked to had different experiences."

"Have you ever met someone from your group. From your coma-group?" I asked Phil.

"Not yet," he responded, "but I probably will someday."

Then, turning around and looking at Krista, he said, "You know, you're actually the fourth person I've talked to that went to Orange-land."

"You call it Orange-land?" Krista asked, grinning widely.

"Yeah, 'cause of the grass," he said, definitively.

"I like that. I've been calling it Coma-Ville. Just to myself, I mean. I've never talked about this with anyone."

"Well, young lady," Phil said, smiling, "I'm always up for talking about it."

She touched her right hand to her heart twice and gave a look of gratitude. Krista was no longer wandering, carrying the weight of having this meaningful piece of her life unshared and unknown. She had been seen. She had been found.

I had so many more questions to ask, but we were pulling up to the airport. After I checked which airlines they were using, Krista asked Phil where he was flying to. San Antonio. A quick weekend trip to see a friend.

I pulled alongside the curb and put the car in park, and then headed to the trunk to get Krista's suitcase, as they gathered their things and exited the car.

For a moment, we all just looked at each other, no one saying a word. It felt like we were all trying to figure out if that conversation had just happened or not. Phil broke the silence.

"Here, let me get your bag," he said to Krista, "I'll walk you to your gate."

Krista stepped aside, allowing me to put her suitcase into Phil's empty hands. Side by side, they both looked at me, as if to get one last glance.

"Wait, Phil!" I exclaimed, "what about you? Where's your suitcase?"

He smiled and slowly shook his head back and forth.

"Listen, friend. When you've smelled joy, and when you've tasted peace down by the cloud river in Orange-Land… …you just don't care about little things like suitcases anymore!"

With that, he grabbed the handle on Krista's bag, and the two of them disappeared into the terminal together.

THE LAST SUPPER

My night almost over, I pulled up to a glossy white apartment building and waited for "Steph plus one" to find their way to the car. The building was one of those new-construction monstrosities that had hundreds of units, rooftop party areas (I assume), and an overly hipster coffee shop on the first floor named "Birch" or "Straw" or some other natural material. Several potential Stephs walked by, but none having a "plus one," unless a yorkie-doodle was getting its own seat.

After about ninety seconds, Steph and the "plus one" (Chad) emerged from the courtyard gate and headed for my backseat, Steph looking back and forth between her phone and my car. She was about five-feet-eleven, with shoulder-length, dirty-blond hair, half of which was pulled back into a ponytail. Her black knee-length skirt had a golden flower design printed on it, and coupled with her short-sleeved, beige button up she looked like she had just gotten off work as an office manager or a bank teller.

Chad was slightly taller than her, thanks to his work boots' thick heels. His loose-fitting jeans were slightly faded but clean, and his white polo shirt was tucked in, showing off his oval belt buckle. His outfit said, "cleaned up construction worker," but I wasn't sure what to make of him. His head was so cleanly shaved that it shined, and his thick, goggle-like glasses created the illusion that his eyes were three times their normal size. Together, they looked too plain for the city, yet they walked hand in hand, confident and comfortable.

As Chad reached for the door handle, I suppressed a yawn and got ready to start the ride, planning to head home after dropping them off.

"Hey Chief, thanks for picking us up," Chad bellowed out, ducking his head in before stepping back to let Steph climb in first.

He had the sort of voice that sounded like he was giving a pep talk or sharing a fun "fact of the day." Like a guidance counselor, or an embarrassing dad. I kept my face turned away from him as I rolled my eyes. I hate it when people use belittling nicknames like "Bud" or "Chief", as if I'm twelve.

"Yeah, no problem" I mumbled in response, already wishing this ride was over so I could go home.

Steph began chatting before her body was fully loaded into the back seat.

"We are so excited! This is our first ever Uber-car!"

By the pride in her voice, you'd think she'd just accomplished something after years of practice, like landing a double backflip or saying the alphabet backwards.

"Oh yeah...?" I mustered up enough energy to sound interested. "Well, what's the occasion? What are you up to tonight?"

Before Steph could answer, Chad shared an enthusiastic note about the sunlight, to which Steph added observations about the gorgeous trees, the lovely singing birds, the heroic cyclists, the humidity, the majestic mountains she saw yesterday, and "just the whole month," whatever that meant. She even shared gratitude for the traffic and crowded crosswalks, staring out the window and speaking to no one in particular.

"Every time I see a traffic jam or all the people walking around, I'm reminded that we're in such an amazing place that so many other people want to be here too!"

The GPS indicated that this would only be a two-mile trip, and I felt a sizable rush of energy, sort of like a marathon runner spotting the finish line (or so I imagine). I heard myself repeat my question about their plans for the night. What came next was worthy of the cliche about drinking from a fire hose, as they explained they were celebrating, and the two of them went back and forth, gushing about life, food, kids, travel, the city, small animals, and anything else that came to mind, while I managed the roads.

Their cute, lovey-dovey routine took approximately eight minutes, which, unfortunately, only moved us 0.4 miles through rush hour traffic.

I was becoming more curious with every passing minute. For some reason, these two were blown away by anything and everything. It was clear they weren't from around here. I guessed that this was their first trip to the city, but by the way things were going, it seemed more like it was their first day on earth!

I finally got a direct answer to my question.

"Well anyway," Steph began, taking a gulp of air, "we've been dying to try this restaurant that you're driving us to, what's it called, Chad?"

"Corliss, I think"

"Cordless, right, just because we don't get to go out on the town very much, but we've heard that this is just the nicest place around."

"Yeah, this whole big city thing isn't what we're used to," Chad inserted, "we live up in Mount Vernon, which is great, don't get me wrong. I mean, we love Mount Vernon."

"Yes, we are so blessed there," Steph whispered in agreement.

I adjusted my rear-view mirror so I could see her face. It was full of life. She had the expressiveness of a mime.

She continued, "Our house is beautiful, and our whole community…" As she let her sentence trail off, I noticed tears welling up in her eyes.

"Just think," Chad interjected, grinning at Steph, "how many people live their whole life trying to find what we've been fortunate enough to have for twelve years now…?!"

I wasn't sure if Chad was asking for a response or not, but it didn't matter because Steph was getting ready for another round. She fought back tears, her voice cracking.

"And our neighbors are amazing, just amaz--"

Her breath caught, and as she continued, her voice was trembling slightly.

"Just amazing. You know, our next-door neighbors, Linda and Sal, they're practically fam--"

Steph paused, tears finally spilling down her cheeks.

"They're family! We just love them so much, you know? They're watching our girls while we're off in the city."

I'm not sure if it was their sheer enthusiasm for life, or the strong emotion that came out in Steph's comments, but something caused me to wake up in that moment, and I shifted from mild curiosity to full-on wonder. Who is so exuberant about pedestrians or birds?! What sort of person is brought to tears by thinking of their babysitting neighbors?! I wanted to know everything about these two.

"You have daughters?" I asked with a small measure of assertiveness.

"Two perfect angels," Chad began, "six years old and almost four. And I tell you what, bud, those little girls are my world. Every day I wake up to the dreamlife, man, seriously! A man can't ask for a better life than this woman here next to me, and our little..." His voice cut out as he choked back tears of his own.

Steph leaned into him as a sort of hug to agree, then took the baton. "How about you, do you have any kids?"

"Uh, yes. Yeah, I have two girls, too." I always cry when someone else does.

Steph pressed for more.

"I bet they're wonderful. Tell me about them! How old are they? Do they make you laugh? Are they reading yet? Do they have you re-read their favorite stories over and over to them?"

Her questions caught me a little off guard. How could I follow the display of love and heartfelt joy that they just put on?! Plus, her interest in me and in my life only seemed to shine a light on my own lack of appreciation for everything around me. Who were these people? Are they like this all the time? Was that even possible?

But then, I started to feel affected by them. Inspired, maybe. I wanted to borrow their perspective on life for a while. Try it on and see how it felt. It had been a long time since I looked at trees with any interest, or the mountains with even the slightest bit of awe. The only thing I felt toward cyclists or pedestrians was road rage, not a sense of affinity. When I brought up my daughters in conversation, it was normally to complain about how early they woke up or how many dishes they dirtied each day. But suddenly, I wanted to drop everything and go hug my family. I wanted to start noticing the world all around me and relating to it with gratitude.

I asked about the apartment where I picked them up. I assumed, since they lived in Mount Vernon, that they were on vacation, and I was feeling energized by how they were living life to the fullest.

"So is the apartment an Air BnB?"

"Well," Steph began with a bit of hesitancy, "Actually, we bought it a few months back."

"Really? Wow. Congratulations."

"Yeah, well we sort of needed a place for me to stay, while... while Chad has been in treatment."

That one word - "treatment" - sucked all the oxygen out of the car and attached a weight to my stomach.

"Oh, I see." I wasn't really sure what I was supposed to say. "What sort of treatment are you getting, Chad, if you don't mind me asking?"

He didn't even blink.

"Well, I have a rare form of blood cancer, so I'm getting some treatment for that."

My thoughts started racing at break-neck speed. Inside my head, the volume got louder and louder.

"Cancer? CANCER?? Wait a second... they have this amazing gratitude and appreciation for everything in life, not complaining about anything and feeling all blessed and stuff... meanwhile he's got CANCER?!?"

"Man, I'm really sorry to hear that," I said, with every drop of empathy I could find. "I bet that's been hard to deal with."

"Yeah, thanks for saying that," he replied. His calm tone made me feel like I had said the right thing. Like I passed.

"You know, it's been a long, difficult road," he continued, "I've had two different stints of chemotherapy over the last few years, but it hasn't really done much. The cancer just kept getting worse."

As I listened to Chad, the weight in my stomach got worse. I thought about what it would be like to be in his situation. There was one thing I knew for sure - if I had cancer, and it was getting worse despite the treatments, I would be angry. I wouldn't be walking around the world feeling grateful for everything. I would be bitter. Furious at the universe's unfairness.

"Chad," I started, still unsure if I was trespassing, "aren't you angry?"

"What do you mean?" He asked.

"I mean, aren't you mad at the fact that you have cancer?"

"Well, sure. I was angry at first. For a while, actually. But you know what? Eventually, I realized that my anger wasn't helping anything."

"Yeah, but it's just not fair," I said.

Chad smiled and nodded, as if he were the one empathizing with me.

"You know what, Bud? You're right. It's not fair. But life's not fair. Instead of worrying about what's fair and what's not, I just try to stay focused on what I can control. I'm taking it day by day."

Steph had her hand on Chad's knee, rubbing it lovingly.

"Chad has been such an amazing example through all of this," she said. "Even the way he's handling this final operation tomorrow."

This conversation had gotten too large for me to keep driving, so I pulled over to a parking spot a few blocks from their destination. I turned in my seat so I could see their faces without using the mirror, and was thrown off by the calm, matter-of-fact expressions that were looking back at me.

"What do you mean a 'final operation tomorrow'...?! What sort of operation?"

Steph explained the situation, almost enthusiastically.

"So, a few months back they took millions of healthier cells from his blood, and tomorrow they are going to blast him with enough radiation to basically kill everything in his body. Then, they're going to put the healthy cells back in his blood and hope that they can successfully re-build his organs and everything."

"That's right," Chad added, "you see, the cancer keeps spreading and growing, so the only option left is to basically wipe out everything. But the blood cells that they took out of me can hopefully do all the repairs before the radiation kills me."

I paused to think about that for a minute. On the one hand, our bodies are kind of amazing, with our billions of cells that all have different jobs and functions and can re-build organs or body parts. And the fact that we have the medical technology to even pull off this sci-fi-like maneuver is really cool. But, on the other hand, I felt sick to my stomach thinking about what Chad was about to go through. And it's not like he did anything to deserve this. He had lived through three years of hell and was about to go through this torturous procedure, all due to the randomness of cancer. Sometimes the world just feels horribly cruel. Evil, even.

I wondered whether it was possibly worse than that, though. I wondered if this operation was risky, and what the chances were that it would work. I didn't know if that was something you should ask, but I was so intrigued by them, I wanted to sit there all night and ask questions.

"Chad, I'm not sure if this is rude to ask, so feel free to answer or not answer, ok?" My voice scratched with every syllable.

"Oh, it's no problem. Ask anything you want!"

"Ok, well… I'm just wondering what the uh… what your chances of, um…"

"Twenty percent," he said, as calmly as if I had asked him the chance of it raining tonight.

"So, there's a twenty percent chance that the operation will fail?"

"No… actually, there's a twenty percent chance I'll survive the operation. And beyond that, there's not a very high likelihood that it'll work."

Chad sighed, and then continued.

"To be honest, and I don't mean to be crass, but… tonight will probably be my last night outside the hospital."

"That's why we are going out," Steph chimed in. "We wanted Chad to get to eat the tastiest meal of his life, and we thought that we should spend our last night together celebrating Chad's life and the amazing blessings we've had and all the beauty and joy and laughter that we've experienced together for the last fifteen years."

I couldn't breathe. I turned back around, facing forward so they couldn't see the tears streaming down my face. I couldn't tell if they were totally insane, or the most amazing examples of what it meant to be human. I wanted to hug them, while at the same time I couldn't handle them anymore. They were overwhelming somehow, invading my core and flipping my world upside down.

I had been happy with my naivety, complaining about everyday first-world problems, but now this was shattering the illusions I used to justify my lack of gratitude. I had seen a different way of being and I knew I wouldn't be able to un-see it. My chest felt like it was on fire and my brain was going into overload.

My mind began running again.

"Let me get this straight. These two have been dealing with cancer and chemo for a few years, and now have this last-ditch operation that will likely kill him, so they decide to go out and celebrate the life they've had?! Where is the self-pity and wallowing?! Where is the despair? Are these people even real?! Is this sort of thing even possible when you're healthy and not going to die?! Or can you only get that perspective if you have something like cancer?"

I had to say something. They were choosing to celebrate on their last night together. What would I be doing if I knew this was my last night on earth? Would I keep driving, sharing life lessons and inspiring every passenger that got into my car? Would I go get my wife and kids and celebrate like these two? Would I sink into my own hopelessness?! (Probably that one)

"Wow... that is amazing. You two are unbelievable. And I know we just met, but can I just say something...?" My voice was shaking so bad, I wondered if they could even understand me.

"First off, thank you for sharing your story with me. I have never heard a story like yours... and I'm really touched...

and moved by it. I was already impressed by the way you both seem to appreciate everything. Like the way you talked about the sunset, and the trees, and the city when you first got in the car. But then, to find out that you have that attitude, all while dealing with cancer and the chance that you might not make it through this operation…?! I mean, I don't even know what to say."

I had gotten louder and louder the more I talked, and wasn't sure if I was coming across right.

I took a breath and then softly added, "I am just so amazed at your resilience and that you both have this perspective on life."

After a brief pause, Steph said, "That's really sweet of you to say. I'm amazed at Chad's attitude every day too, and I just really do feel fortunate that we've had so many awesome experiences."

Then, after watching her finish the sentence, taking in every word she said, Chad added the response that broke me.

He said, "You know, I wouldn't trade my life for anyone else's in the world."

I allowed my tears to run freely, doing everything I could to avoid full-blown sobs. Putting the car back in gear, we drove the final two blocks in silence.

How do you say goodbye to someone you've just met, who is, statistically speaking, most likely going to die in the next few weeks? Every parting line I practiced in my head over the final few seconds either felt inappropriate for two strangers, or too trivial for the situation.

I wanted somehow for our relationship to continue on after the ride ended. I wanted to visit Chad in the hospital. I wanted to meet their kids and introduce my kids to them. I wanted to sit somewhere and ask so many more questions. And what I wanted the most was to find a way to cure Chad from his cancer.

As we pulled up to the restaurant, I put the car in park and turned around again in my seat. Steph's smile seemed to acknowledge all of those things that I wanted and reassure me that things would be OK. Chad held out his hand for a shake.

"This was the best Uber we've ever had," he said with the smile that follows corny jokes and puns.

I shook his hand, looked him in the eyes, and let out a sigh.

"I know you're going to think that I say this to everyone, and I don't; but I will *never* forget you two, or this conversation. I think I really needed to meet you tonight."

Steph put a hand on top of our handshake, like a sports team's huddle, and Chad gave my hand a squeeze.

"Goodbye, Chief," he said, as he opened his door.

Somehow, I felt complete. His goodbye had closed some circuit. I watched them walk away from the car, hand in hand, ready to face whatever would come next. Then I succumbed to one of the hardest cries of my life.

Acknowledgments

I must begin my acknowledgments with the elephant in the room: these weren't my stories to tell. I was gifted the opportunity to craft a story-mirror, that might give others the chance to glimpse what I had a front-row seat to as a rideshare driver. The people behind these stories are remarkable and I consider myself privileged to be the one to introduce you to them.

To the real Ali, Clint, Gary, Timmy, Nathan, Heidi, Amal, Miranda, Krista, Phil, and Steph - I'm beyond grateful that you shared your true selves with me. Thank you for allowing me to share your brilliance with the world.

To the real, late Chad - I wish I could have showed you what the book came to be. You're the reason it exists, and your words are still inspiring us. Rest in peace.

To the thousands of passengers not mentioned in this book - thank you for graciously indulging me in conversation, singing karaoke, creating a page in the rider journal, keeping me from running over that pedestrian on 15th Ave, playing telephone-hangman, helping me change that woman's flat tire, sharing your pizza with me, inviting me out on the town, becoming my mentor or a best friend, letting me use your bathroom when I had an emergency, suggesting I sleep over (I was flattered), asking my advice on your relationship, acting like you weren't a world-famous soccer star, teaching me all about Iceland, and everything else that happened in that car. Five stars to you all.

It took a village to bring this book to life. What began as an idea for a single story in 2016, grew to nine stories, written over six years. And I had a lot of help along the way. Thank you to my early readers for your feedback, to my community of writers and friends for the encouragement which kept me from giving up dozens of times, and to my fellow storytellers for enhancing my love of this craft.

To Tracy Simpson - I love every piece of art you create, but none more than this awe-inspiring showstopper. I'm eternally grateful that you've graced my book's cover with it. If anyone is still reading this (bless you!), do yourself a favor and explore the intelligent, tasteful collection of her work at www.tracy-simpson.com.

Finally, to Katie, Zoe, and Kya - My life is already a smashing success because I have you three in it. Thank you for supporting me all along the journey. Thank you for always wanting to hear another tale. Thank you for making me feel worthwhile. I love you.

About the Author

Andrew Spink is a storyteller. Through his work as an author, solo-show performer, comedian, and public speaker, he curates journeys through the human experience that examine our beliefs, tickle our sense of wonder, and spur us on toward meaningful living. He lives in Seattle with his wife and two daughters, where he feels guilty for not being outdoorsy, avoids coffee while frequenting cafes, and walks his dog to fit in with the crowd. Follow Andrew's work at his website:

AndrewSpink.com

Let's Keep in Touch

This book is just the start of a conversation. If you enjoyed this short-story collection, please consider giving a review online, so other potential readers can find it. And, if a story or two in this collection was meaningful to you or ignited something in you, Andrew would love to hear from you. He reads online reviews, and he responds personally to all communication sent through his website.

About the Cover Artist

The cover art is a bespoke printing, created using russet potatoes, by the phenomenal Tracy Simpson.

Tracy is a Seattle-based printmaker who often finds that her art returns to certain themes over and over – time, layers, loss, injustice, endurance, hope. Her work begins with a penciled grid covering rag paper, and then she uses the smooth face of cut russet potatoes to place acrylic paint on paper, usually after making an impression in the paint from textured fabric or a dried leaf or flower or discarded bits of paper or cardboard. She typically layers the stamped shapes to create a sense of depth and to play with the ways colors behave when they are intersecting with one another. You can find more information and see some of her recent work on her website:

www.tracy-simpson.com